LORDS AND GENTLEMEN

BY

LOUISE HALL THARP

PICTURES BY

CHARLES V. JOHN

1940

THOMAS Y. CROWELL COMPANY

NEW YORK

1: A SHIP COMES IN

A CROWD of ragged children were gathered on Billingsgate Wharf in London. They were quarreling over who should be "it" in a game of tag. "I was not caught," shouted Peter. "Bess should count out all over again."

> "Barber, barber, shave a pig,
> How many hairs to make a wig?"

Bess began, and one by one, the children dropped out.

> "Four and twenty, that's enough,
> Give the barber a pinch of snuff."

The lot fell to Peter after all, but he did not mind. "That was fair, anyway," he declared. He cocked his head on one side, and his bright eyes gleamed with mischief. Then he darted among his playmates, who ran screaming in all directions. Peter singled out the biggest boy, a bullying sort known as Tom Chucklehead. Tom might be big, but Peter Cutler was the fastest runner on the waterfront. A few breathless turns around a high pile of bales, and Tom was caught.

> "Can't catch a flea,
> Can't catch me,"

cried Peter. He dodged and twisted in and out among this crowd of children who were his friends. London docks were his only playground, but he loved the noise and confusion. Sometimes he got in the way of a hurrying dock hand, who aimed a blow. But Peter dodged—most of the time. Sometimes a rope broke, and a heavy bale fell right in Peter's path. He escaped—somehow.

But there was something Peter Cutler cared for more than all the life of London's busiest wharf. Peter loved ships! He would have sailed away from London any day, on any ship, if he could have persuaded a captain to take him. Even now, he turned his back upon his playmates and climbed one of the great wooden piles that formed a corner of the wharf. Here he perched to watch the river.

And the Thames was really a sight worth seeing. Although the water-men declared that 1635 had brought even more of those new hackney coaches, most of the London traffic still flowed by on the river. "Westward Ho" someone would shout and the water-men would come clamoring for the passenger. Or if the cry were "Eastward Ho" the boatmen knew that someone wished to go up stream. But Peter paid no attention to mere water-men, or even to barges. His eyes were always on some tall vessel, finding her way in from foreign ports. On she would come with the flooding tide, her square sails set, her high gilded poop gleaming in the sun. Peter would laugh to see the water-men's little boats darting back and forth almost under her fore foot. They were like impudent street boys in the path of a great lady. He tried to imagine the storms the ship must have weathered; the strange lands she must have seen.

Below, on the wharf, the game of tag changed to hide and seek, then back to tag again, while Peter watched the river. Bess stopped by the piles where he was perched. "Now then," she shrilled, "you big booby! What you gawkin' at? Come along and play." She reached up and tweaked his bare toes.

Peter pulled his foot out of reach. "Let me alone, Bess," he said. "I'm tired of your game. Look at that Norsey out there! I'll wager she's coming in at our wharf."

Bess glanced out at the river in the direction Peter was pointing. "Who cares!" she exclaimed. "What's a 'Norsey,' any-how?"

"A 'Norsey' is a North Sea barque, as anybody ought to know," Peter replied. "Maybe they're small but they'll sail anywhere. Look how that one handles. There's a good man at the tiller, too. Watch how he lets the tide bring her in. Why, that barque could cross the Atlantic."

Bess laughed. "To the New World you're forever talking about, Peter? Why that boat's no better than a wherry! Peter, you're daft. All you talk about is going to sea. You'll drown, dunderhead. I'd liefer swing by the string than drown."

" I was right," exclaimed Peter, ignoring her remarks. "They are coming in here, sure as fate. Can you make out her name?"

3

"As if I could read!" jeered Bess. "I knew a woman who could read, once. She was burned for a witch. Come on, Peter —play. Don't mix yourself in gentlefolk's affairs."

But Peter did not move. He could read the name on the boat, now. *"Bachelor,"* it said, in rather faded letters.

There were passengers on board, and the other children began to take an interest in the approaching vessel. Passengers sometimes tossed coins to ragged children who amused them. Two of the boys began to turn cartwheels. Peter would have liked to stay where he was, but he could not afford to miss a chance to earn a little money, so he began to do balancing tricks on the edge of the pier.

There was a lady on the boat, wearing a dark green traveling cloak. Peter saw that she was watching him. She spoke to a broad-shouldered man who stood beside her. Peter turned a somersault, pretending to fall in the water and catching himself just in time. The lady laughed. Pleased with his success, Peter was about to play the trick again when Tom Chucklehead came along, shoved him aside, and took the center of the stage for himself.

Peter was not at all dismayed. He stuck out his tongue behind Tom's back, then climbed the pile of woolsacks, and began to imitate all of Tom's tricks. This made the other children laugh and point at Peter, while Tom imagined that the applause was for himself. Tom exerted himself to do more and more tricks, till he grew red in the face and out of breath.

Peter, however, had been watching the passengers on the barque out of the corner of his eye. The lady was amused, but she did not throw the boys any money. The man by her side must certainly be a soldier; he had the resolute air of one ac-

4

customed to command. He did not seem to be particularly impressed by the children's tricks. "That's a man who will pay for service, but not for foolishness," thought Peter shrewdly. "If I can manage to help him with those boxes of his, I shall get some copper—but that's my only chance." Peter climbed off the stack of wool, and began to edge his way toward the spot where he knew the gangplank must fall.

The other children saw what he was doing, however, and they were quick to guess his plan. They needed pennies nearly as badly as Peter did, so when the gangplank was finally lowered, all the children were crowding around. Tom, being the biggest, soon shoved his way to the front.

But Tom was too confident. He was so sure of being first on board the boat that he forgot to watch where he was going. Quick as a flash, Peter's foot shot out in front of him, Peter's fist caught him off balance, and the next thing Tom knew, he was in the muddy water. Peter ducked under the arm of a sailor who was clearing the way for the passengers, and ran up the gangplank before anyone could stop him.

"Carry your boxes, sir?" he asked, politely pulling off his rag of a cap. "You're for the King's Head Inn, sir, I hope. The best on the river."

"Have they sent you from the inn!" exclaimed the gentleman. "Yes, I am going there, but they should have sent two men, at least. Look at my boxes! You're not big enough to carry one, let alone all!"

"I'm twelve," said Peter, drawing himself up to his full height, and looking straight into the keen, gray eyes of the stranger. To Peter's annoyance, he saw a twinkle of amusement in those eyes. He doubled up his thin arm to show his muscle.

5

"I'm very strong," he declared, "just try me!"

"I'm very strong," he declared, "just try me!"

At this point, there came a shout from the jetty, as two stalwart men appeared, scattering the children from their path. "Here come the other porters from the inn now, sir," said Peter with dignity. "We shall manage easily."

Tod and Perkin, the porters from the King's Head, came trotting up the gangplank. Tod aimed a blow at Peter, in passing. "Run, Nipper," he said. "Keep out of our way. You'll get a beating. Mutton's burnt. Cook's looking for you."

Perkin pulled his forelock respectfully to the passengers. "Sergeant Lion Gardiner and Lady?" he asked. "We're from the King's Head Inn, sir. There's a hackney coach for you at the top of the stairs."

The men shouldered the boxes, and started off. Peter felt as discouraged as a boy of his cheerful disposition could ever be. He had told Sergeant Gardiner the truth when he said he had come from the King's Head Inn. The trouble was that he should never have left the place. He was supposed to turn the spit for the cook. He had stood beside the great stone fireplace and turned the spit too, until his face felt roasted, even if the mutton were not. Then Cook left Peter alone for a moment, and Peter promptly ran off to the wharf to play. He slipped away every chance he got, and he stayed away until hunger drove him back. He got a good, sound whipping and precious little to eat, whenever he turned up at the inn again. But the play and the sight of the ships were worth the pain.

This time Peter thought he might escape a whipping if he came back bringing a fine gentleman's boxes. Just as the plan seemed about to work, Tod and Perkin had to come and spoil it. Peter kicked at a coil of rope with a disconsolate air, and tried to think what to do.

A pleasant voice startled him out of his gloomy musing. It was Mistress Gardiner speaking. She had turned back, and now stood at his side. Peter thought she was the most beautiful lady he had ever seen. She had pale gold hair and blue eyes, and she spoke with a foreign accent. She pointed to a little leather-covered box, with the initials "M. W." done in brass nail heads on the lid. "Could you that box carry, boy?" she said. "Could you be careful, please?"

"Of course," cried Peter, eagerly seizing the box and putting it on his shoulder. "Anything else? Let me take your cloak for you. It's a hot day, even for August." The lady took off her long woolen traveling cloak, and gave it to Peter. He saw that her dress was of green silk, with a broad lace collar and cuffs, such as court ladies wore. He was very much impressed, and stood staring at her admiringly, until he noticed that Sergeant Gardiner, who waited at the head of the gangplank, was laughing at him. Peter flushed, and started after the lady in his most dignified manner.

Behind Peter came the little barque's other two passengers: a sturdy middle-aged man in coarse clothing, and a rather sharp-featured woman carrying an elegant dressing case. "That's the lady's maid," thought Peter, "but the man is not a valet; he's too big and rough-looking. Might be a workman. Tom Chucklehead's a fool to offer to carry his box. That's a man with no coppers to spare."

"So you needed a porter of your own, did you, Mary?" Peter heard the sergeant say. "Well, you picked a smart little rap-scallion." They climbed the steep and slimy stone stairs that led into Fish Street. Mistress Gardiner lifted her skirts and stepped

8

carefully, her face a picture of dismay at the mud and refuse that lay all about. Her husband laughed at her. "Not much like your clean, neat Holland, is it?"

"Then the lady is Dutch," said Peter to himself. He loved to learn all he could about people by watching and listening. "The sergeant is certainly English, though," Peter thought. "Could he be something of a Puritan? His clothes are very plain."

They came out on a street so narrow that the tall, half-timbered houses, which jutted out a little further at each story, nearly touched each other at the top. They had once been handsome, but now fashionable London was moving up the Thames beyond the bridge, and the old houses were falling into disrepair. They leaned toward each other like aged crones whispering scandal of bygone days.

The waiting coach practically filled the roadway. It was fortunate these lumbering vehicles were still scarce, perhaps, for had another one come along, the two could never have passed. Mistress Gardiner looked up Fish Street and gasped. "Why I never saw a hill so steep!" she cried. "Is it safe? How can a horse pull a coach up a hill like that? He will fall down."

"The horse won't fall, unless he falls asleep, my dear," laughed her husband. "I suppose the hill does look steep to one accustomed to such a flat country as Holland. Get in—don't be afraid."

Just at this point, a terrific squealing and barking broke out, and down the street dashed four young pigs, with a large brown dog close behind them, nipping at their heels. Mistress Gardiner leaped into the coach without another word, but she leaned out the door to watch the pigs go by. Her face was so full of shocked astonishment that Peter almost burst out laughing.

He hopped up on the step of the hackney. "Don't they have pigs in Holland, ma'am?" he asked, curiously.

"Oh yes," she replied, "but we keep them in pens. Somebody have just lost the pigs—yes?"

Peter laughed. "Oh, they didn't get loose, ma'am; they just live in the street. At Christmas time there are not so many, because they are caught and eaten. The soldiers of the guard always get the biggest."

"Are the guardsmen allowed to own pigs?" exclaimed Sergeant Gardiner, suddenly becoming interested.

"Oh no," said Peter. "They take the best because they wear swords nearly as big as yours, sir."

"I see," said Sergeant Gardiner with a chuckle.

But now angry shouts and more loud squealings were heard. The two other passengers from the barque *Bachelor* had been walking up the street behind the hackney coach. Peter looked back in time to see the man thrust the woman against the wall of a house, put down his box, and begin to lay about him with the flat of his sword. It was the pigs again! This time there were more of them. They had been turned at the waterfront by another mongrel dog, so they dashed madly back up the street, right in the path of the foot passengers.

Sergeant Gardiner leaned out of the coach. "Well done, William Job," he shouted, roaring with laughter. "Have at them. A thrust—a parry—now a parry in tierce, my man! That will confound them." As the hackney coach climbed the hill very slowly, the sergeant had plenty of time for humorous comment. "Shall I come to your aid, Job?" he cried, "or can you save the fair Eliza single-handed?"

William Job was getting very red in the face. The flat of his sword came down on the fat sides of the biggest pig, and the resulting squeals could be heard for miles. That ended the conflict, for the other pigs all ran off after their leader.

"Hush, Lion, stop teasing poor old Job like that," gasped Mistress Gardiner, wiping tears of laughter from her eyes. "Look at Eliza," she cried with a fresh burst of merriment. "The girl has flung her arms around her hero. Now William Job is wishing he had the pigs back again, instead!"

Sergeant Gardiner leaned back in the coach. "The Battle of the Pigs," he muttered. "How bravely we begin our venture!"

They reached the King's Head, turned, and rattled into the inn yard. Peter jumped down and opened the door of the coach with a flourish. He could see the cook watching him from the low dark doorway across the court, where stables and kitchens stood. He was very glad he had that little trunk to carry up to the room assigned to the guests, which was on the other side of the courtyard.

You can put off an evil moment only so long, however. Mistress Gardiner was looking down into the courtyard, while her maid, the still slightly breathless Eliza Coles, began unpacking her boxes. "There goes my little porter, Eliza," she said. "Isn't he a clever little chap?" Then suddenly, she cried out in dismay, "Oh!—oh what a shame!"

A man wearing a greasy apron had slipped up behind Peter, grabbed him by the collar and was beating him unmercifully. "H'm," said Eliza, coming to the window, "I dare say the little rascal deserved it. But that man is laying on the stick a lot harder than he needs to!"

Mistress Gardiner turned from the window with a sigh. "I wish there were something we could do for that boy," she said.

11

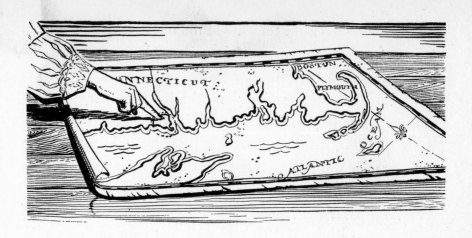

2 : THE COMPANY OF LORDS
AND GENTLEMEN

A MAN in a red velvet cloak thrust open the door of the King's Head Inn. He glanced about the taproom, and his eye fell on Peter, who was sanding the floor. "Boy, is this the place where Sergeant Gardiner and the Company of Lords and Gentlemen will meet?"

"Yes, sir," said Peter briskly. "They have engaged our best room. Shall I show you?"

"What ails the boy?" thought Hobbs, the innkeeper, sourly. "Here it is, a fine August morning. The door to Fish Street has been open a dozen times, and yet he has not tried to run away! He is a likely enough lad when he has a mind to work. That's the tenth fine gentleman he's shown into that parlor as elegant as if he'd been around the gentry all his life. They'll be giving him silver for his pains pretty soon. But I'll see to that!" Here, the innkeeper rubbed his fat hands together. "I'll see who gets the money in the end," he promised himself.

But Peter was not planning mischief, nor was his mind entirely on tips. There was a big map spread out on the table in the private room, and gentlemen were gathered around, examining it eagerly. Peter caught a glimpse of bays and promontories, boldly drawn in black ink on the crackling parchment. Names were picked out in red, with many a flourish. What coast line could it be? What were those names? Peter was consumed with curiosity.

With the arrival of the red-cloaked gentleman, who was greeted as Mr. Fenwick, it was plain that the business in hand was about to begin. Peter's new friend, Sergeant Gardiner, took a seat at the head of the table, and ranged all along the sides were gentlemen of evident wealth and consequence. Opposite the sergeant sat a plainly dressed young man whom the others referred to as "our agent, Mr. Hopkins."

Peter listened eagerly when Sergeant Gardiner spoke. "This Connecticut, as you call it, Mr. Hopkins—what does the name mean?"

"That is Indian language," Mr. Hopkins replied. "I am told it means 'long tidal stream.' This map we have before us is a copy of one made by the late Captain John Smith, but how many miles long the river really is, we do not know. The Indians who bring beaver skins down in canoes speak of 'many days' journey.' "

Peter's eyes sparkled. "Indians! That means America," he thought. "These men are planning some brave venture in the New World, where they will surely make their fortune. Oh, if I could only join them! I would follow that long river and be

Peter was consumed with curiosity.

the first white man to reach its source. I'll wager I'd find gold, and come back as rich as King Charles." Peter's idea of the resources of the New World were wildly impossible, but older heads than his had been filled with similar romantic dreams before him. He longed to ask questions, but he knew that if he said a word he would be sent from the room for impertinence.

Mr. Fenwick was examining a large imposing-looking document with many red seals. "So this is your charter," he remarked. "How much land does His Majesty grant you?"

"We have a thousand and five hundred acres at the west side of the river's mouth," Mr. Hopkins told him. "If you decide to put your money in this venture, Mr. Fenwick, we will build you a fine house in our city." Mr. Hopkins opened a paper showing streets and plots, all neatly drawn. He laid this plan on the table beside the map. "You should come in with us at once, or all the best locations will be taken. Outside the town, you can buy up as many acres as you like for your plantation. At present, the price is most reasonable, you know."

"But how fertile is this river valley?" Mr. Fenwick asked.

A small man at the other end of the table sprang up. "I can answer that question," he cried. "Listen!" He pulled out a paper and began to read. " 'There grow there naturally a store of black wild vines which make very good vinegar. There is also great store of deer and buffalo, which may be ridden and brought to plow. The spring waters there are as good as small beer, here.' "

"Why, where did you get that paper, Mr. Simpson?" exclaimed Mr. Hopkins. "May we all see it?"

"My sister sent it from Holland," Mr. Simpson exclaimed. "The Dutch are flocking to 'New Netherlands,' as they call it,

16

and this is what they write of the country. Surely they will take up all the best land, unless we build our fort at once, and claim our river."

"It is true that the Dutch do lay claim to the Connecticut," said Mr. Hopkins. "It's some ridiculous nonsense about a man named Block; they say he was the first to sail up the river. Our English Captain Smith discovered it first, of course. Sergeant Gardiner's fort will soon make the Dutch see reason."

Mr. Fenwick still appeared to hesitate to join the venture. "Tell me," he said, "has Lord Saye and Sele really become a member of your company?"

"Yes indeed," said Mr. Hopkins, taking a letter from a pile of papers before him. "Here is his signature. Lord Brooke has also joined us, and bought a considerable share in the company. In fact, we consider naming our city 'Sayebrook' in honor of these two gentlemen."

"Very suitable," exclaimed Mr. Fenwick, evidently much impressed. He hesitated no longer. "Consider me a member!"

"Splendid," cried Mr. Hopkins. He jumped up, shook hands with Mr. Fenwick, and produced a paper for him to sign.

"Now," thought Peter, "why don't they all drink to the success of the venture or something, so I can have a chance to serve them? Old Hobbs will soon catch me in here doing nothing, and I'll be sent to help the cook." These were very sober gentlemen, however; no more orders were forthcoming.

"Why don't you sail with Sergeant Gardiner, Mr. Fenwick?" Peter heard Mr. Hopkins say. "I could arrange very good accommodations for you on board the *Bachelor*."

"The *Bachelor!*" exclaimed Mr. Fenwick. "You want me to cross the Atlantic in that cockle shell? I should say not!"

17

"Oh come," said Mr. Hopkins, "she's a fine, sturdy little vessel. How about you, Mr. Simpson? The price of a passage would be reasonable."

"Well—er—thank you, Mr. Hopkins, but I've seen the *Bachelor* tied up at the wharf. Really, I think not. It would be expecting too much of God's Providence for a boat like that to make the crossing safely."

At this point Peter's fears were realized. He was hustled off to work, as he expected. "The *Bachelor's* a good little ship," he said to himself, as he started to sweep the kitchen floor. "I'd sail on her any day."

At last, the inn began to quiet down for the night. The tap-room was empty, and most of the lights went out upstairs. Cook stumbled off to bed, and Peter was free to curl up in the straw in a corner of the stable, where he usually slept. He did not go there, however. He had seen the gleam of a candle which was still burning in the room the Gardiners had taken. Peter stole up the stairs.

When he reached the door, he waited a few minutes before he found courage to knock. A poor scullery boy had no business coming to a gentleman's room, and he knew it. "Still," thought Peter, "if he sends me away and tells old Hobbs, I'll just get another beating, that's all. It's worth the try."

Sergeant Gardiner answered the knock. "Could I speak to you a moment, sir?" said Peter.

"Why, it's my little porter," exclaimed Mistress Gardiner, looking up from a table where she had been writing. "Do let him come in, Lion. What's the trouble, boy?"

Peter stepped into the room and closed the door. "I came to

ask if you need a servant, sir, to take with you to America. I am
not afraid to sail on the *Bachelor,* and I would join the venture,
sir, except I have no money. If you would let me serve you and
the lady, I would work for nothing as long as you like—just to
get to the New World."

Peter had been talking as fast as he could, for fear of being
sent away before he had said his say. Now, he paused for breath
and looked hopefully at Mistress Gardiner. She smiled kindly
at him and spoke to her husband. "Oh, do you think we could?
We've both spoken of how they treat him here. Only he's so
young!"

"I'm afraid your father would never let you go, my boy," said
Lion Gardiner. "He seems to find plenty of work for you right
here at the inn."

"My father?" questioned Peter, puzzled for a moment. Then
he understood. "Oh, the innkeeper is not my father, sir. Oh no!
They say my father is dead; at least Mr. Hobbs came and told
me my father was dead, and I—well, I suppose it's true."

"Tell us about it," said Sergeant Gardiner gently.

"Yes sir," said Peter, "—only some things I don't remember
very well. Before we came to London, we had a farm. Then the
Lord of the Manor said we couldn't use his land any more. He
built a fence. He said he was going to keep sheep, because you
can get a good price for wool. I don't understand much about
that, except father said we must have land if we were to live.
There's plenty of land in America, isn't there, sir?"

Sergeant Gardiner nodded.

"That's what father said," Peter went on. "So we sold everything except the things we could carry to—to the Plymouth

colony, I think they called it. We came to London, and paid most of our money to go on a ship.

"But—well, this part is hard to remember. Mother said some-one told the king's men we used to have people come to our house on Sundays. It was true. All our neighbors used to come and talk about the Bible. I remember because mother made me listen, but I used to fall asleep. Anyway, the king's men came to the inn and took my father. Mother said they put him in prison.

"Mother was very brave. She was sure father would come back. We let the ship sail without us, and they wouldn't give us back our money. The innkeeper kept wanting money, too. We sold the rest of our things.

"We waited and waited. Mother tried to find where they had taken father, but no one would tell. She worked for Mr. Hobbs so we could stay at the inn. She was afraid that if we went away, father would never find us. After a while, she caught a fever. People said it was the plague." Peter swallowed hard, then went on. "Before mother died, she gave me a little picture of herself she had. Do you know the kind? It was painted in pretty colors, and it had a silver frame." He looked at Mistress Gardiner.

She nodded. "I know—a miniature."

"Yes," said Peter—"that was it. I was to give it to father when he came for me. Mother always said that he would come. But Mr. Hobbs took the miniature and sold it. He sold all our things. He said we owed him money, so the things were his.

"Mr. Hobbs has let me stay here ever since. But he says father will never come, and now I begin to think so, too.

"So, if you please, sir! I would work very hard."

Sergeant Gardiner took a turn or two up and down the room.

20

"What's your name, boy?" he asked abruptly.

"Peter Cutler, sir, of Amesbury—or I used to be from Amesbury."

"When did they take your father away? Can you remember?"

"It was eight years ago," said Peter, thinking aloud. "Because I was four, and now I'm twelve."

"Oh, couldn't you try to find out about Peter's father?" begged Mistress Gardiner.

Her husband looked doubtful. "We have so little to go on," he said. "These arrests are kept secret, you know. The bishops grow more and more powerful, but they are still careful not to anger the people over-much. Haven't you some relatives in Amesbury, Peter? You should write a letter."

Peter hung his head. "Mother taught me to read," he said, "but I have nothing to practice on, except the names of ships. I'm—I'm afraid I can't write at all."

"I will write for you a letter," cried Mistress Gardiner. "But you must tell me what to say. My husband says I make English into Dutch, when I talk. So you will help me—yes?"

Peter smiled. "I like the way you talk English, ma'am. But I don't want to write a letter to my aunt."

He turned to Sergeant Gardiner. "My relatives wouldn't want me. Mother said we must never go back—they wouldn't have us. So will you take me with you, sir?"

But Sergeant Gardiner shook his head.

3 : PLANS FOR PETER

PETER supposed that the *Bachelor* would sail at once, but weeks went by and she still lay at her wharf. He seized every opportunity to get aboard her, for he liked the little ship uncommonly well.

"Hey, Nipper," shouted a carter one morning, "seen a ship called *Bachelor?*"

"Right here," said Peter, pointing down the dirty steps to the wharf.

"Well, take this to the captain, will you?" The man fumbled in his pockets and pulled out a soiled paper.

Peter took the paper joyfully. It meant another chance to get on the barque, and with a really good excuse this time. He found Captain Webber at his breakfast. "Cargo at this hour," the captain grumbled. "Hopkins isn't here, and neither is his clerk. Who's going to check this list, I'd like to know?"

"I could check it, sir," said Peter hopefully.

The captain seemed to see him for the first time. "You, again," he exclaimed, not too cordially. "Well, bring the quill and the ink pot then, and we'll see." He strode on deck, shouting to some sailors to "bear a hand and look alive, can't ye!" Hogsheads and barrels were soon piling up on the deck. "Twenty barrels of meal," counted the captain rapidly.

"Check," said Peter, marking an item on the list, as he had seen warehouse clerks do many a time.

"Fourteen of peas."

"Check."

"Oatmeal—one. Six firkins of butter."

But before Peter could say "check" to the last item, there came a scraping, then a bump on the far side of the ship that nearly threw him off his feet. The captain's face turned purple with rage. He strode to the rail, breathing hard. "Belay there," he shouted. "You walrus-eyed son of a sea cow. Get that mud scow of yours off the side of my ship, or I'll—" Here, the captain launched into a string of abuse so violent and so varied that Peter was filled with admiration.

The bargeman, however, did not seem impressed. "Got the whole Tower of London to come aboard," he said, grinning and adding a few oaths of his own.

Peter looked curiously at the load. There were chains, bolts and bars of iron—a formidable pile, to be sure, but what had it to do with the Tower?

"Ahem! Pardon me!" Peter turned to see who was trying to speak to the captain, and there stood Mr. Hopkins, the agent. That puritanical gentleman was evidently so shocked by the

23

captain's language that Peter burst out laughing.

"So you've come at last," growled Captain Webber. "Here is the ironwork for the fort on the river. Hooks for the portcullis, chains for the drawbridge. It's all here."

"Now I understand," thought Peter. "Sergeant Gardiner is going to build a castle like the Tower of London. Won't it look splendid in the New World! There'll be a drawbridge right across the Connecticut, I expect."

But Peter was not left long to his romantic imaginings. "Here, boy," called the captain—"Where's my list? Where did I leave off?"

"Six firkins of butter was the last item," replied Peter promptly.

The captain looked at him with just a hint of a twinkle in his frosty blue eyes. "You're the boy that's always pestering me about wanting to join my ship, aren't you?" he said. "Well, you're too young, as I told you before, but you made yourself useful today, so now go to the galley and ask Cook for a meal."

Peter did not have to be invited twice. He ran to the galley, where a good-natured Portuguese gave him a better dinner than he ever got at the inn. Afterwards, he wandered over to the rail to watch his friends playing on the wharf. He hoped they would think he was a real sailor at last.

"Ho there, Peter," shrilled Bessie, when she saw him. "They are making a great outcry at the inn for you. You're hunted high and low."

Peter grinned. "Of course," he said, "but I'm not hungry, so Cook shan't get his hands on me yet awhile."

"Not the cook—the lady wants you," said Bess, standing on the edge of the wharf, and looking up at Peter with something

24

very like respect. "The fine lady with the yellow hair is even sending her serving wench about to look for you. She says—" here Bess paused dramatically—"she says you have a letter!"

Peter threw back his head and laughed. "Oh Bess," he cried, when he could get his breath, "nobody ever sent me a letter, and you know it."

"I didn't believe it, either," said Bessie, feeling relieved.

But suddenly, Peter remembered something. A little less than a month ago, Mistress Gardiner had written a letter for him to his aunt in Amesbury. So it could be— Peter walked slowly down the gangplank. "All right, Bess," he said absently, "I suppose maybe there is a letter for me, at that." Bess stared at him, struck speechless for the first time in her life.

Peter listened in silence while Mistress Gardiner read his letter aloud to him. When she finished, he still had nothing to say. "Are you not happy, Peter?" inquired Mistress Gardiner, speaking slowly and carefully, so as not to make mistakes. "Your aunt says that she wishes it that you should come at once."

"Excuse me, ma'am," said Peter, and his jaw took on a stubborn look. "My aunt says she supposes she'll have to have me. She doesn't want me at all—and I don't want to go there. I want to go to America with you."

There came a knock at the door. Sergeant Gardiner entered, followed by a man in a plain, gray cloak. It was Mr. Hopkins, Peter remembered—agent for the Company of Lords and Gentlemen. "Oh there you are, Peter," said Sergeant Gardiner. "You have good news in your letter, I hope?"

"My aunt says there are mouths enough to feed in her own family, sir, without me," said Peter. "She doesn't want me, so

25

Bess stared at him, struck speechless for the first time
in her life.

can I go with you? I can clean boots, polish saddles—"

"May I see the letter?" Peter handed it over. He noticed that Mistress Gardiner was talking to Mr. Hopkins. They glanced his way now and then, and Mistress Gardiner looked sad.

"H'm—not very cordial, I'll admit," said Sergeant Gardiner, handing back the letter. "But she'll take you, so that's where you go, young man. I can't be bothered with a mere child in the wilderness."

Peter opened his mouth to speak, then shut it again. There was no use arguing with a soldier, and he knew it.

Sergeant Gardiner saw the look of misery in his eyes. "Cheer up, child," he said kindly. "Work just as hard for your aunt as you would for me, and she'll be glad you came, after all. Now, some of the gentlemen you have been waiting on here at the inn have given me money for you. They knew that Hobbs would take it from you if he saw them hand it to you in the taproom." Sergeant Gardiner took some silver from a purse, and began to count it. "Here is enough for your fare in the coach to Amesbury. It leaves from the Three Cups Inn in St. John's Street. You go up Long Lane, through Charterhouse Yard and along Charterhouse Lane—but I forget; you are a London boy now. You probably know the way as well as I. Here are three crowns over and above the fare on the coach. I think that is enough to buy you a decent coat, if you've a mind."

"Did you speak to Mr. Hopkins about—about father, sir?" asked Peter.

"Mr. Hopkins is here to tell you about that himself, Peter. I'm afraid it's bad news, my boy."

Mr. Hopkins came forward. "Your father's name was Robert Cutler; is that right, boy?"

27

"Yes, sir," said Peter.

Mr. Hopkins showed him a paper. "I have managed to get a list of prisoners for the year 1627. Here is a Robert Cutler, charged with heresy in the spring of that year."

"And what is heresy?" asked Peter. "Is it something very bad?"

Mr. Hopkins smiled slightly. "In the eyes of the king's bishops, it is very wrong. You see, the king and the bishops believe that everyone should belong to their church. They feel certain that it is wrong for ordinary folk to read the Bible. Now, heretics are people who go to churches of their own, and believe they have a right to do so. Did your father have a Bible in his home?"

"Yes," said Peter. "He kept it hidden away from some of the neighbors, mother told me. And he did not go to the king's chapel, either."

"So, you see, your father was what the bishops call a heretic, although I call him a brave man," said Mr. Hopkins. "I would like to have known him."

"Then—then you did not find my father in prison?"

"No, he is not there. I have searched for him as thoroughly as I dare. I, too, am a Puritan, Peter, so I have to be careful. I might find myself in a cell, charged with heresy, too. It is not easy to get a look at prison records, but I have done so. There is no record of his death—nor of his release.

"I have questioned the turnkey who should have known your father. But even with the help of a little silver, he remembers nothing. There was the plague, Peter. Records were not kept very well at that time. I am afraid there is no doubt but what your father is dead."

Peter realized that he should thank Mr. Hopkins for his kindness—but he could not speak. He turned his face away, so that no one should see his tears. "I'm too big to cry," he thought —but he couldn't help it.

Sergeant Gardiner looked helplessly at his wife. "I don't know anything about children. Would it cheer him up if you took him out to buy a new coat?"

"Oh yes," exclaimed Mistress Gardiner, as pleased with the idea as any child could have been. "Eliza—my cloak! And my hat with a plume upon it. Peter, go call us a hackney coach."

Peter had stolen many a ride on the back of a hackney coach, but he had never been inside of one. He opened the door for Mistress Gardiner with a flourish that would have done credit to Mr. Fenwick of the red cloak and the silver-hilted sword. But as they left the inn, he saw Tom Chucklehead climbing on behind the carriage. Peter could not resist the temptation. He stuck his head out of the window and thumbed his nose.

"Peter!" exclaimed Mistress Gardiner.

Poor Peter blushed scarlet and mumbled an apology, but then he saw that she was laughing. "Oh I don't like that little black mask across your eyes," he said. "I can't tell if you are angry with me, or not."

"I do not care for it, myself," said Mistress Gardiner. "I think it is a queer fashion." She took off the domino as she spoke, and turned it about curiously. It was made of silk, stiffened with buckram. There were narrow slits for eyes, and it was stitched around the edges very prettily. "I have heard that the beautiful little Queen Henrietta has this style from Paris. All the court ladies wear the mask in London. My maid says I will be called a 'bare-faced hussy' if I go on the street without

29

one." She sighed, and fastened the mask in place again. "We do not wear these things in Holland," she added, "and I think in the New World, where there is no Court of King Charles, I shall not need it, either."

All this time, the hackney had been taking them up Fish Street, and along the river. Now the great fortified gate of London Bridge came in sight. Above the battlements were poles on which the heads of traitors had been placed. It was a gruesome sight, but so common that little attention was ever paid to it.

"Have you been here before, Peter?" asked Mistress Gardiner.

"Yes," said Peter. "The night Mr. Hobbs found where I had hidden mother's miniature, I followed him, and he took it here and sold it to a silversmith. Do you see that little shop over there? That's the one. I thought I might somehow get money enough sometime to buy it back, but I never did."

They left the coach at the bridge gate, and crossed the street to look into the tiny leaded glass window. "The man must have sold it long ago," said Peter sadly, "but I'd rather have it than a coat, any day." He straightened the ragged garment he was wearing. "This is a pretty good coat," he declared.

"Let us go in," said Mistress Gardiner. "I will ask to see some silver shoe buckles."

The shopkeeper looked very suspiciously at Peter, for there were plenty of ragged street boys in London who stole whatever they could lay hands on. He brought out buckles and bracelets for the fine lady, however, bowing and smiling obsequiously.

"Have you any old silver?" Mistress Gardiner asked. "I do

not like these buckles very well, but perhaps I will like a—what you call a locket, maybe."

The man brought out a tray full of more or less tarnished trinkets, and she began to turn them over. Suddenly Peter tugged at her sleeve and pointed to an oval silver case at the bottom of the pile. She picked it up, and glanced at him. He nodded. Then Mistress Gardiner proceeded to bargain for the miniature so cleverly that even Peter himself was not sure she meant to buy it. She asked the price of this piece and that. When the silversmith finally sold her the old silver-framed miniature for six shillings, he thought he had been very smart.

"And you still have enough money for a coat," whispered Mistress Gardiner, as they left the shop. She put the little silver locket in Peter's hand, and he held it tightly. It felt just the way he remembered it had.

They stopped at several shops having second-hand clothes for sale. Mary Gardiner came from a shrewd Dutch trading family, and she loved to strike a good bargain. She found two coats, either of which would do. "This one is very good for the country, Peter," she said. "Look—it is dark-colored, and neat for to wear when you to church go. This other is too warm, I think—but such a bargain! Maybe your aunt those brass buttons will cut off. They would make you look—well, too much like a sailor."

That was exactly what Peter had been thinking. "Oh could I have the blue?" He spoke softly, for fear the shopkeeper might raise the price if he betrayed too much enthusiasm. "I could polish those buttons till they are as bright as Captain Webber's."

"But the good Aunt Martha is a Puritan lady, is it not so?"

31

began Mistress Gardiner. Then she looked at Peter's face, and turned abruptly to the shopkeeper: "I take the blue," she said.

When they were back in the coach, Peter put the miniature into Mistress Gardiner's hand. She looked at the picture—then at Peter. "You have her eyes, I think—yes? Your mother must have been very sweet." She held out the locket, but Peter shook his head.

"Would you please keep it for me? I lost it once, you know, and I'm afraid someone will take it away from me again."

"But Peter, I will soon be far away across the sea."

"Yes, of course—but if you don't mind keeping it awhile, I will come to Saybrook for it."

Mistress Gardiner looked into Peter's earnest face. "I believe you will, Peter," she said at last. "Very well, then, I will the little picture keep for you—until you are a man."

"It might not be as long as that," said Peter, grinning impishly. But when Mistress Gardiner tried to make him tell her what he meant, he would not say another word.

32

4: OUTWARD BOUND

"NOT another wheelbarrow, I tell you!" shouted Captain Webber.

"But Captain," Mr. Hopkins protested, "wheelbarrows fetch double their price in America. You have left but one aboard. And look at these grindstones! Why, you have unloaded all but six, according to my list."

"If I load one more wheelbarrow, another grindstone, or even a feather bed, my ship would founder," Captain Webber declared. "I know agents. You care nought for our lives! But consider your goods sir. Give rein to greed, and you lose all."

"Very well, very well," said Mr. Hopkins, "have your way, sir. Do you sail with the ebb tide?"

"I do, sir."

"I will take horse at the inn, then, ride down the river, and meet you at Gravesend with your clearance papers. Good day." Mr. Hopkins strode off with annoyance manifesting itself in every swing of his long, gray cloak.

Sergeant Gardiner turned to his wife with a sigh of relief. "Good," he exclaimed. "We should, God willing, have a successful voyage, for it is plain the master of this barque knows his business. Look! The tide is beginning to turn, already. Take your farewell of London, Mary. We are bound for the New World at last."

Mistress Gardiner smiled. "At last," she echoed. "I like your London—yes. But our Saybrook I like more." They strolled along the tiny deck of the *Bachelor,* and paused to look down at the wharf. "I rather thought our little Peter would be here to say good-by."

"Oh, he's forgotten all about us already," her husband replied. "Don't adopt every stray unfortunate you meet, Mary; you will have your heart broken too many times."

Mistress Gardiner smiled to herself. "He is just as fond of Peter as I am," she thought. "He feels just as sad to leave the boy behind."

But now, with much shouting and running up and down, the ropes were cast off, a sail was hoisted, and the wharf grew small in the distance.

Back at the King's Head Inn, a stranger was calling for Hobbs, the innkeeper. "I've come for Mistress Cutler and her son, Peter," the man said. "Where are they?"

"But—but that lady is dead, sir, this long time," stammered Hobbs in amazement.

The stranger sat down in the nearest chair. He had turned

34

very white, but after a moment he asked, "When—when did it happen?"

"Oh, 'twas the plague, sir—three or four years agone. Surely you remember. Business was at a standstill. The king would not come nigh to London. Oh, but 'twas soon over; not a very bad plague. Only the poor lady took it and died quite sudden like. Did you know her, sir?"

The man sat with his head in his hands for a moment, unable to speak. Then he looked up. "But the boy—the little chap? Did he die, too?"

"Lord bless you, no, sir; the boy is hale and hearty. He's round here somewhere. Indeed, I've been like a father to him, sir. In fact, I'm badly out of pocket for the young lad's keep. So if you're a friend of his, or a relative, maphap—" The innkeeper paused expectantly. But the man only nodded.

**The stranger sat down in the nearest chair;
he had turned very white.**

35

"Yes, yes—send for the child."

"Peter!" shouted Hobbs. There was no answer. "Excuse me, sir; I'll fetch the dear lad." Hobbs waddled out. "Where is that brat, Peter?" he demanded when he reached the kitchen.

"Why, he's off to the Three Cups Inn," the cook replied. "Jerry got the story out of the lady's serving wench, after the little wretch himself had run clean off. Those gentlemen he's been waiting on have given him a purse of money, and he's off for Amesbury on the evening coach."

"I'll teach that limb of Satan to run off like that," cried Hobbs. "After him, Jerry! Bring him back here, right away. And bring me the purse of money, do you hear?" Hobbs went back into the taproom rubbing his fat hands together and smiling. "The dear child is off at play. I have sent for him. Now, I will just make up the tally for his keep."

In about half an hour, Jerry came hurrying back. "Yes, yes," said Hobbs. "Now send the brat privately to me, while I tell him what to do and say. Give me the purse, and if there's anything gone— What are you standing there with your mouth open for, you oaf!"

"Peter wasn't there!" stammered Jerry. "I ha'n't got him, Mr. Hobbs."

"You mean you missed the coach!" cried Hobbs, seizing a stick.

"No, no! The coach was still standing at the inn door. I searched it from top to bottom. I made a great outcry—I said the lad was wanted by the King's Justice. I cried out he had a stolen purse on him—all to no avail, sir. The boy was just— not there!"

"Ye did well," muttered Hobbs grudgingly. "If he'd a been

there, ye'd have caught him. Where can the child have got to!"

Hobbs went back to the stranger with lies and excuses. He tried his best to get this man to tell his name, and his business with Peter. "H'm," thought Hobbs shrewdly, "Here's a man who's in London at his peril, I'll be bound. If I can find the wretch Peter, this man will buy the child of me for a goodly sum. He seems set on having him. If Peter comes not back by sundown, I'll have in a sergeant of the guard to look at my close-mouthed customer. Maybe there's a price on his head."

Just before sunset, however, the stranger suddenly left the inn. He was in the street before Hobbs missed him. There, a ragged little girl pulled at his cloak, to beg from him. He shook his head; but then he seemed to change his mind, for he asked her a question.

"Aye, to be sure, I know Peter," Bessie told him. They talked together for some time. "Well then—I do know where he is, Mister," Bessie said at last. "I think you speak truth, or cross my heart, I wouldn't tell. Lean down while I whisper."

By this time the barque *Bachelor* was tied up at the wharf in Gravesend. There was a smell of the sea in the air, and the little ship seemed like a bird impatient of her bondage, longing to be free. She was far from free, however.

As Mr. Hopkins stepped aboard with letters, clearance papers and part of the seamen's pay, four men approached him. John Brinken, the carpenter, stepped forward. "We want leave to stay in the New World, sir," he said. "Put it down on paper that we can have the wages due us in Boston—not back in London."

"The Winthrops won't like this," thought Mr. Hopkins. "They want only Puritans, whose faith is exactly like their own,

37

to stay in Boston."

He turned to the seaman. "Now now, my good man, your contracts read that you are to return to London. This demand of yours to stay in Boston is ridiculous."

"Maybe," said John Brinken, truculently. "You write a new paper for us, just the same, or we jump ship right here in Gravesend."

Mr. Hopkins knew there were no sailors to be had in Gravesend, so he was forced to give in. He went to the captain's cabin to draw up new contracts. "How many men stay with the ship, Captain Webber?" he asked.

"My mate and I, and one sailor. But I own this barque, as you know, and I do not expect to sail her back to London at once. I shall first see what offers in the way of coastwise trade among the colonies."

Mr. Hopkins groaned inwardly. "Another newcomer the Winthrops will not approve of," he thought. "Very well," he said. "How about the cabin boy?"

"He's helping the cook in the galley, but I have his word that he will stay with me."

The new contracts were finally drawn up, and thirty shillings paid to the men. Then the river pilot was paid off. The *Bachelor* was free to sail at last.

Mr. Hopkins mounted his horse, ready to ride back to London. He lingered a few minutes beside the wharf, however, watching the *Bachelor's* tiny white sail grow smaller in the distance. There was a stiff breeze blowing, and she heeled over and drove along briskly. Mr. Hopkins sighed. "God send her safe to port," he thought.

He turned at the sound of a horse galloping down the road.

A man rode up to the wharf in great haste, dismounted, and hurried over to a small vessel which was just leaving. It was the *Abigail,* bound for France, a sailor told him. So the man turned, and came back to the road. "I beg pardon, sir," he said, noticing Mr. Hopkins for the first time, "but can you tell me if the ship *Bachelor* has reached Gravesend?"

"She has just left, bound for the Bay Colony. If you look, you may see her, down the channel."

The man looked where Mr. Hopkins pointed, and his face became so pale that Mr. Hopkins was alarmed. "Are you ill, sir?" he exclaimed. He got down off his horse. "Come into the inn with me; let me help you."

"You are very kind," said the stranger, allowing himself to be led into the taproom close by. "I was sure that I would find the *Bachelor* here, and when I saw I was too late—" He sank into a chair. "I am better now," he said presently. "Come to think of it, I have not taken time for food for many hours." He called the landlord and ordered a simple meal.

"I believe I will sup here, too," said Mr. Hopkins, for he had taken a liking to the stranger, and wanted to learn more about him. He thought the man might be a Puritan like himself, for his clothes were extremely plain, his gray hair was cut short, and his hat was without a plume.

"My name is Robert Cutler," said the stranger. "I am—er— from Amesbury."

"And my name is Edward Hopkins—of London. But this is a coincidence. I have been searching for a Mr. Robert Cutler— but not in Amesbury."

"Where, then?"

"In Newgate Prison!"

39

Mr. Cutler half rose, as if to leave. Then he sank back in his chair. "Very well," he said. "I make no doubt I am the man you seek. I am from Amesbury, but more recently, I escaped from Newgate Prison. Friends urged me to hide in the country, but I came to London seeking my wife and child. I have just learned that my wife is dead, after what hardships and sufferings I dare not think. I was told that my son is cabin boy aboard the *Bachelor*. I know not if this is true. In any case, I have small chance of ever finding him now. So if you have been searching for me, to take me back to prison, pray do so. Perhaps I shall have a fair trial this time—though I doubt it."

"Softly, sir! I beg you!" exclaimed Mr. Hopkins. "I am no king's magistrate. Hush! Do not say these things aloud. Here comes the waiter with our supper."

The two men ate in silence till they were left alone in the taproom once more. Then Mr. Hopkins spoke in low tones. "I am a Puritan, like yourself—so you have nothing to fear from me. I sought you for the sake of a boy, Peter Cutler, your son, I think? When I was sure you were not in Newgate, it seemed certain you must be dead. So Peter's friends arranged for him to go to Amesbury."

"His friends!" exclaimed Robert Cutler. "It does my heart good to hear you say that he had friends. I talked to a little playmate of his who told me that my Peter was beaten and abused."

"That is true, too, I am afraid," said Mr. Hopkins. Then he told Peter's father all he knew about the boy, and about the Gardiners who had wanted to help him.

"So he is in Amesbury, and I shall go there at once," said Mr. Cutler. Then he hesitated. "But the little lass, Bessie, really thought my boy was aboard the *Bachelor*. Tell me, did you

40

chance to see the cabin boy?"

"It is strange, but I did not," said Mr. Hopkins. "I saw only a few mutinous fellows who demanded changes in their articles. The boy was not among them." He took a paper from an envelope. "Here are the names of the seamen."

Mr. Cutler read the paper over. "John Harman, John Hall, Robert Sherley, the boy," it said. There were all the seamen's names, except the boy's. "If only you had seen him, sir!" he exclaimed. "I shall go to Amesbury, but if my Peter is not there, I must somehow find means to reach the New World."

"You have plenty of time," said Mr. Hopkins. "The *True Love* is the next ship sailing for the Bay Colony, and she leaves no sooner than a month from now. Let me know, and I can arrange accommodations."

Mr. Cutler smiled sadly. "My accommodations, sir, will be most meager. A man does not spend eight years in jail, and come forth wealthy. I cut the buckles from my shoes and sold them to hire that horse, yonder. I have little enough left now, but in Amesbury I have friends and relatives. I shall either find my Peter there, or find the means to follow him wherever he has gone."

The man's gentle, yet resolute face had such a look of hope and confidence that Mr. Hopkins held out his hand. "Good luck to you, sir," he said. "Let me know how you fare."

They rode back to London together. Then Mr. Cutler took the road to Amesbury.

5: THE NEW WORLD

SERGEANT and Mistress Gardiner were seated at table with the captain, when they felt the little ship begin to rise to the ocean swell. Now the great adventure had really begun. They smiled at each other. The cabin boy came in with a steaming platter of food. Mistress Gardiner glanced up at him as he passed the plates.

"Look!" she cried, seizing her husband's arm excitedly. "It's our Peter!"

Peter took his place behind the captain's chair as though he had been a cabin boy for many voyages. He had polished the buttons on his new blue coat till they shone nearly as brightly as his mischievous black eyes. However, the look of surprise

42

and disapproval on Sergeant Gardiner's face made Peter feel suddenly much less pleased with himself.

As soon as his duties at the table and in the cook's galley were over, he sought out his friend. "Here is the money you gave me, sir," he said, tugging at the purse, and finally drawing it out of his back pocket. "I know it was just for my fare to Amesbury in the coach. I'm not going to Amesbury, so I think I ought to give it back."

"I see you are not," said Sergeant Gardiner, dryly. "But if you think you are going to Saybrook with me, you are very much mistaken. I only take men who obey orders."

Peter flushed. "Yes, sir," he said. "I would have obeyed you, except I got to thinking how my aunt hated to have me on her hands. So I managed to run errands and do odd jobs for Captain Webber till I showed him I knew how to work. When he signed me on at last—I—well, I almost told you, sir. But then I was afraid you'd make me go to Amesbury, so I hid out till we were at sea."

Sergeant Gardiner had been counting the money Peter had handed him. "I see you're honest, even though willful," he said, looking a little less severe.

"I used four shillings," said Peter, "but I paid them back out of my advance in wages. I bought trade goods in London, sir; six fish hooks, two knives and a package of needles. I get eight shillings more in Boston, and then Captain Webber and I intend to trade among the savages."

Sergeant Gardiner suppressed a smile. "In business for yourself—h'm. Well Peter, this money was given you because of your services to certain gentlemen. I think it is still yours, even though you did not use it for the purpose intended." Sergeant

Gardiner handed the purse back to Peter. "A trader must have capital," he said.

Peter knew that his disobedience had been forgiven. "I have promised to stay on the *Bachelor* with Captain Webber for a year," he told the sergeant. "After that, if you need a good man at the fort, sir——"

The sergeant laughed. "You never give up an idea, do you, boy?" he remarked. "Well, let me see what a smart, hardworking cabin boy you can be. Then, learn all you can about trading. After that, we'll see; we might make a soldier out of you yet."

The *Bachelor* had left Gravesend on the eighteenth of August. The eighteenth of September found her wallowing along in a welter of gray sea. "How can Captain Webber tell where we are?" exclaimed Mistress Gardiner. She had been very miserable with sea sickness at first, but she was over it now, and she walked on deck every day. She always looked for Peter, and when he was not too busy, they walked together.

"Oh, Captain Webber is a fine navigator," said Peter. "Why, with good fortune, we should sight land in about two more months!"

"Two whole months! Why Peter, that means we'll be three months at sea. Is it not so?"

"Yes ma'am, but that's very good—for a Norsey," said Peter, defending the boat he loved.

William Job, Sergeant Gardiner's master of works, came stumbling up the companion-way to the deck. "Don't tell poor Will how long the voyage will be, Peter," whispered Mistress Gardiner. "He drives us mad with his complaints." Peter promised readily enough, but he knew he could not resist teasing Job

44

whenever he got a chance, for Job gave himself airs toward sea-men, and detested small boys.

William Job had come on deck with Sergeant Gardiner, and Peter paused on his way to the galley to hear what they were saying, for the word "fort" caught his ear. "Of course I cannot draw you a plan of the fort today," Sergeant Gardiner told Job with considerable impatience. "I must see the spot to be forti-fied; you know that as well as I."

"But if you could give me some idea, I could be turning it over in my mind, like," mumbled Job.

"You'll be able to build me what I want when the time comes. Now stop worrying."

"Do you trust that Mr. Hopkins, sir?" persisted Job. "Has he put everything on board what we're going to need? Them solemn-faced gentry sometimes cheats, sir."

"Of course Mr. Hopkins is honest. What will you think of to worry over next? Go count the cargo, if you think it will do any good."

Sergeant Gardiner never expected Job to take this sugges-tion seriously; he was merely relieved when the man took him-self off.

But William Job stopped at the galley to borrow a candle, and then climbed down between the decks of the *Bachelor*. Peter saw him go, and followed, full of curiosity. Job was dis-appointed to find most of the cargo deep in the hold, impossible to reach. A few kegs were lashed to a stanchion near the foot of the ladder, however. "Forty staple hooks" was scrawled on the top of one, and after some difficulty, Job got this keg free of the others, opened it, and began counting the contents. After a while he looked up and found Peter watching him. "Get out of

45

here, you young monkey," he shouted. "Thirty-three, thirty-four—drat it all, I've lost count. Go away, brat, and stop bothering me."

Peter leaned over, and blew out the candle. Then he snatched three hooks from the keg, and hid. Poor old Job was so angry that his hands shook and he was a long time lighting the candle with his flint and steel.

Job assumed that Peter had gone, so he set to work counting the hooks again. "Only thirty-seven," he exclaimed. "It's just as I thought. We've been cheated." He rushed on deck to tell Sergeant Gardiner. Of course, while he was gone, Peter put back the missing hooks.

"There's nothing to be done about it now, William," said the sergeant wearily. "I do wish you wouldn't bother me about the fort till we get there."

However, since Job was so distressed, he went below decks to look at the hooks. Job counted them again—thirty-six, thirty-seven, thirty-eight, thirty-nine, forty. Poor Job's face was a study in bewilderment. The sergeant laughed, and went back up the ladder. "Now that will teach you not to worry, Will," he said.

Job sat down by the keg and began to lay out the hooks in sets of five. "There should be eight—eight fives," he muttered. Peter crawled across the planks, keeping out of the candle light, took a hook away from one pile and added it to another. William Job's head was in a whirl. Peter had to cover his mouth to keep from laughing. He was just reaching for another hook when Job caught sight of him.

Job let out a roar of rage, and Peter sprinted up the ladder. "That boy," puffed William Job, following "—stealing my

46

Peter ran up the mast, behind the seaman,
to watch for land himself.

hooks, was he? Just wait till I get my hooks on him!" He heard
a mocking laugh which seemed to come from the clouds. Peter
was up the mainmast, sitting in the crosstree. "I'll get you, yet,"
shouted Job, shaking his fist. But he knew all too well that Peter
would probably get the better of him, instead.

The days went by with very little to distinguish one from another. The food grew scarcer and less palatable. Friends had
insisted that the Gardiners carry lemons and limes with them
to prevent scurvy, and Mistress Gardiner made Peter share
them. They seemed a very strange fruit indeed to Peter. He had
seen them for sale in London, to be sure, but only rich people
bought such things. The weather grew increasingly cold, and
the blue coat which had seemed so warm when Peter bought it
in London, was now of hardly any use in keeping out the wind.

One morning Peter found the captain marking the ship's po-
sition on the chart, so he stopped to watch him. "How close the
land looks on the map," he remarked. "Look at that long head-
land called—" he paused to puzzle over the letters—"called
'Cape James.' It looks like a skeleton hand with one bony finger
beckoning to us."

"Belay that talk of skeleton hands," ordered Captain Webber. Then he added, half to himself, "I've heard about that spot.
The settlers call it 'Cape Cod.' It's a dangerous place. Unless we
give Cape Cod a wide berth, we'll all be skeletons before our
time, and that's a fact. Run up on deck, boy, and take a look at
the glass."

"She's falling, sir," reported Peter.

"Mr. Baker," shouted the captain from the foot of the companion-way.

"Aye, aye, sir."

"Set another lookout in the crosstrees, mister. Tell him to look sharp for land on our port bow."

Peter ran up the mast behind the seaman, to watch for land himself; but he soon came down again, it was so cold.

When Peter first woke the next morning, he wondered why he felt so comfortable. Then he realized—he was no longer very cold. He hurried on deck, expecting to see some miracle of warm sunshine. Instead, the whole world was white. Sails had been reefed during the night, but the bare poles were white-coated. A wall of twisting, whirling flakes closed in around the ship. A half-frozen lookout clung to the mast, but he could see nothing. With the coming of the snow, the wind had also died down, which was great good fortune. "How close to land are we now?" Peter asked anxiously.

"As if I knew," growled the mate. "Pipe down and get breakfast ready."

Peter had seen snow before, but never anything like this storm, which lasted all day. He had learned enough about navigation to realize that the ship was much too near an unknown shore for comfort. He listened to the monotonous voice of the leadsman, calling out the soundings. There seemed to be plenty of water, but who could tell when it might shoal off suddenly?

"Hark for the sound of breakers, young 'un," said one of the sailors. "If you hear 'em, sing out—but pray God there's nought to hear."

Peter listened, but he could hear nothing but the creaking of the cordage and the soft hiss of snowflakes as they hit the water. He wanted to watch and listen all night, but he was ordered below to get some rest.

When Peter awoke, the air was bitter cold again, and he

rightly guessed that the snow was over. He rushed on deck, and there along the western rim of ocean, gleamed a pure white coast. Peter rubbed his eyes and looked again, but it was not a dream. The frozen land was really there. He gave a shout of joy, and rushed below to tell the news.

The next few hours were full of excitement and Peter was sent dashing up and down on so many errands, he had hardly time to watch his new land draw near. Toward afternoon, however, he noticed that the coast, which had seemed at first to be flat and straight, was now deeply indented. They were running into a large harbor. At its head were three low hills.

When Peter got another chance to look, he could make out a few houses. "Can that be Boston!" he thought with considerable disappointment. He had expected to find a smaller town than London—but this was hardly a town at all!

6: SHORE LEAVE

THE *Bachelor* crept cautiously forward, feeling her way with the rising tide. Small islands rose here and there, covered with fresh fallen snow. Peter thought they looked like cakes piled high with dazzling white icing. He sniffed the air with delight, for it had a clean, frosty smell that he had never known before. The sky was a brighter blue than English sky can ever be, and Peter felt a strange sense of elation mounting within him. He wanted to toss his cap and shout for joy.

But now the shore was near, and a stout little dory could be seen, with a man in it rowing vigorously toward them. "Pilot ahoy!" shouted Captain Webber hopefully.

"Captain John Gallop, at your service, sir," roared the hearty, red-faced individual at the oars. The rowboat was made fast to the *Bachelor*, and Captain Gallop climbed aboard. "First and only pilot of Boston harbor," he said, shaking hands with Captain Webber. He looked at the little barque. "I don't believe you'll need to anchor in the roadstead, the way the larger vessels do. There's water enough for you at the wharf side." He took the wheel. "Pretty rough voyage?" he asked.

"H'm, not bad," Captain Webber said, noncommittally. "Do you often have heavy snowfall like this, so early in the year?"

"First time we ever had the like," replied Captain Gallop. "Snow knee-deep on the twenty-eighth of November! Why, even the Indians say it's uncommon! 1635 has been a hard year, sir, and 1636 will be no better!" Captain Gallop's cheerful red face belied his pessimistic tone, however. As he steered the little ship among rocks, islands and huge ice cakes, he threw out his great chest and began to sing in a deep voice. It was a psalm tune that he sang, but he made it sound like a sea chanty.

When they tied up at the wharf, it seemed to Peter that everyone had liberty to go ashore except himself! Sergeant and Mistress Gardiner were met by a man whom they greeted as "Governor Winthrop."

"Not governor, now," the man corrected them. "Thomas Dudley was chosen governor just a few months ago. I am plain John Winthrop, very much at your service."

William Job had his box all corded and ready on the deck. Eliza Coles beckoned coquettishly to him to follow her, but he had been looking over the side of the vessel toward the wharf. "No, no!" he exclaimed. "Look there! Savages!"

Among the group of colonists who had gathered to greet the *Bachelor* stood two Indians, who were quietly watching what must have seemed to them a very large canoe. Each was wrapped in a blanket against the cold, and, to Peter's disappointment, they carried no weapons. "Don't pay any attention to those Indians, my man," laughed Mr. Winthrop, who had noticed Job's dismay. "That's old Cutshamakin and a friend of his. They're Narragansetts, and perfectly harmless."

52

But Job was not to be reassured. "No," he declared, "I am not going ashore. When I was a lad, I ran away to sea, but one voyage was enough. I know all about natives in foreign ports. If the savages don't knife you, then there's dancing girls and strange drinks, and you wake up in jail!"

Sergeant Gardiner looked at the group of sober, gray-clad Puritans gathered on the shore, and laughed. "No dancing girls, Will. They don't allow such things. Just look at them."

"What! Are they all long-faced, psalm-singing gentry, like that Mr. Hopkins? I don't believe it! There never was a foreign port like it. I'd wake up in jail."

"Some people have all the luck," thought Peter. "Old Job can go ashore if he wants to, but he won't. I'd go like a shot— and they won't let me."

Next day, however, the coveted shore leave was granted. Peter made straight for the highest of three hills that rose above the village. "From there," he thought, "I shall really see this new country of mine." He followed a winding street that led past a few frame houses. It twisted and turned, for it was originally a cow path—but it did not lead to the top of the hill. Peter left the road, and struck out through the snow. In a few minutes he heartily wished he had chosen some other direction. He had managed to get hold of an old pair of shoes on board the boat, but his sailor pants let in the snow around his ankles, and his feet soon felt like lumps of ice. He had no cap, and his ears hurt.

Suddenly he heard footsteps behind him, and, turning, he saw a big boy coming up the hill, pulling a little sledge full of fire wood. The boy seemed to be a year or two older than Peter, and how Peter stared with envy at his clothes! He had a fine fur

cap with a fluffy tail hanging down his back, and his legs were snugly wrapped in leather.

"Hello," said Peter. The boy grinned pleasantly. Just then the sledge struck a rock under the snow, and one of the split logs fell off the top. Peter picked it up and put it back. "Thanks," said the boy. Peter took hold of the back of the sledge, and helped push it up the hill.

"My name's Sam West," the stranger said, as they stopped a moment to rest; "what's yours?"

"Peter Cutler. I'm a sailor off the *Bachelor*."

"I'm a fisherman myself," said Sam, "when I'm not a wood-cutter," he added with a twinkle.

"The wood is for the beacon." Sam pointed to a pile of rocks, the purpose of which had been puzzling Peter. "It's easier to haul it up here over the snow. In summer the road is full of ruts."

"And what is the beacon for?" asked Peter.

"Oh, to give warning of danger. We would light a big fire. The settlers would see it for miles, and they would all snatch up their guns and rally at the Common. It might be Indians attacking us, it might be the French, or maybe the Dutch. Who knows! My two brothers are sentries up here from April till the end of September. They started in last March when the town voted to pay a guard. I'm glad I didn't get the job. Too dull!"

"It wouldn't be dull if the Indians attacked," said Peter.

"Oh, but they won't. Narragansetts are all friendly. They like to trade with us too well to fight."

Peter was glad to hear that. They began to unload the wood

**The next thing he knew,
they went flying down the hill.**

together and stack it near the beacon. As Peter turned toward the sledge, he saw a little girl running up the track in the snow, toward them. She wore a thick, full skirt that came down to her ankles, a warm little jacket and a knitted hood pulled snugly over her ears. Her cheeks were bright pink from the frosty air, and her big, gray eyes were sparkling with mischief. When she noticed that Peter had seen her, she put her finger over her lips and shook her head. Then she hid behind the beacon. Peter

55

grinned, but said nothing. It was evident that Sam had not seen the child at all. "Who is she?" Peter wondered. "She looks as if she would be fun to play with."

"Now I'll show you some sport," said Sam, when the wood was all stacked. "Get on the sledge behind me."

"Me, too," cried a laughing voice, and the little girl came running out from behind the beacon, and jumped on the sledge.

"Sally," exclaimed Sam. "How did you get here! Get down at once! What will mother say?"

"Mother won't say a word, unless you tell her," said Sally, with a giggle. She settled herself a little more firmly on the sledge. "Come on—give me a ride, Sam."

"All right," said Sam, "but you must go straight home when we get to the bottom of the hill. If anyone sees you and tells mother you've been up to tomboy tricks again—well, you know what will happen. Come on, Peter."

Peter balanced on the back of the sledge, and the next thing he knew he went flying down the hill. Sally squealed with glee, and Peter shouted. He thought it was the most exciting ride he had ever had, but Sam seemed dissatisfied. "Snow's too deep," he grumbled. "If we had a track packed down, we would go much faster."

"Well then, let's pack it down," cried Peter, delighted with the new sport.

"I ought to get another load of wood before sundown," said Sam doubtfully, but he began to work on the path. One or two other boys joined them after a bit, and Peter was having so much fun that he almost forgot the cold. "Oh, this is much better than London," he thought.

Sally set to work, too, when she saw that her brother had for-

56

gotten to send her home. "What's your name—Peter what?" she said, smiling. "Where do you come from?"

"Oh, are you a real sailor?" she cried in admiration, when Peter told her. "I saw the *Bachelor* from my window, the day she came in. Mother wouldn't let me go down to the wharf, of course."

"Can't you ever come to the wharf?" asked Peter. "I would take you on board the *Bachelor*—that is, if you like boats."

"Oh, would you!" cried Sally, her gray eyes lighting suddenly. But then she shook her head. "Mother would never let me. Girls must stay at home, you know."

Now the snow track was finished, and the children tried it out with shrieks of delight. There was only Sam's sledge, but one of the other boys had a splendid idea, or he thought so at the time. He ran into the tiny school house that stood near, brought out one of the new pine benches and turned it bottom-side up to make a sled. This worked so well that the others ran shouting for benches. In no time the little school was empty, but the hillside was noisy with coasting children.

Suddenly one of the boys shouted, "Look out! The Magistrate!" Peter did not know exactly who "the Magistrate" might be, but experience had taught him to run when boys shout "look out." He ducked around the stack of firewood, and then peered cautiously out to see what was happening.

A tall, very grim-looking man in a high-crowned hat had caught one of the boys by the coat collar, and was laying a heavy staff across his back in a manner all too familiar to Peter. The other boys were running off in all directions, but when the man called upon them by name to stop and come back, they did so, to Peter's surprise.

57

Not far from Peter's hiding place stood little Sally West, her face full of terror. The magistrate had not seen her yet, so Peter darted out quickly and pulled her back of the wood with him. "Oh," she gasped, her eyes full of tears. "What shall I do? Mother will never forgive me."

"Run," said Peter. "Follow me. Don't just stand there and cry, you ninny!" He cut back along the far side of the hill, making for a lane. To his relief, Sally ran fast after him.

When they reached the lane without being seen, Peter paused for breath behind the lean-to of the nearest house. But Sally was still frightened. "Look," she said, pointing the way they had come. "Our tracks in the snow! We can't stay here— they'll find us."

"Tracks," said Peter to himself. "This is something new. We never had to worry about tracks in London." He snatched her hand, and pulled her over a fence.

7: PETER THE WUNX

PETER leaped from the top of the fence into the middle of a narrow path which someone had shoveled in the snow. Then he turned to Sally, who was still clinging rather precariously to the palings. "Can you make it?" he asked anxiously.

Sally jumped, and, in spite of her long skirts, she cleared the snow bank nicely. "Not bad—for a girl," said Peter. He grinned as she landed in the path beside him. "They can track us to the fence now, but they won't be sure which way we turned. Come on! This path leads around the house. The sooner we're in the road, the better."

The children started to run, but to their dismay, they saw the house door ahead opening slowly. They turned, and dashed back down the path and into the barn. It was dark inside, and surprisingly warm.

Now it was Sally who knew what to do. "Hide in the hay," she whispered, pulling Peter into what looked to him like a black hole. It proved to be a springy, slippery mound, sweet-smelling, but hard to climb. Peter had barely time to draw his feet up out of sight when the barn door opened.

"Now that's a queer thing," he heard a man's voice mutter. "Door's open. I must be plumb careless, lettin' in the cold like that. Or did you open that door, Tom Tucker?"

As there was no answer to this question, Peter could not resist leaning forward a little to see who the two people might be. To his surprise, the man was none other than Captain Gallop, the harbor pilot. And as for Tom Tucker, he was a big, gray cat! But Peter's movement, slight though it was, caused a rustling in the hay. He heard Sally draw in her breath with apprehension. Captain Gallop stopped short, and looked over at the hay mow. "We're caught," thought Peter, and he prepared to make a rush for the barn door. He waited a moment more, however, and it was just as well he did.

"Hear that, Tom Tucker? That's rats, and you're a lazy, good-for-nothing cat," the captain said. Tom Tucker paid no attention to these reproaches. Perhaps his big, yellow eyes, so keen in the dark, had already seen the children. He arched his tail, and trotted just ahead of the captain. Soon the children saw the reason for Tom's expectant air. Captain Gallop had come to milk his cow, and the big cat had learned to sit up and let his master squirt a stream of milk into his mouth. Peter had never seen a sight like that before, and he almost laughed aloud.

His amusement was brief, however, for he heard Captain Gallop remark, "Now then, Bossy, some hay, I suppose." The captain strode over to the hay mow and pulled down a big fork full. He came so close to the children's hiding place that they could feel the hay quiver all around them. Another fork full like that, and they would surely come tumbling down, right at the captain's feet. They tried to crawl farther back, but their motions made a dreadful rustling.

"I've a mind to run those rats out of there myself," the captain declared. "That might teach you a lesson, you big loafer. You're the laziest deck hand I ever shipped." Tom Tucker rubbed against the captain's legs and purred. "That's right, 'Little Tommy Tucker sings for his supper,' " quoted Captain Gallop. "But he won't get to work and catch a good supper— not he! Well, come along." The captain picked up his pail and went out, closing the door carefully behind him.

At last the children dared to breathe. "Oh," whispered Sally, "I was sure he'd find us—weren't you?"

"Yes," admitted Peter. "I was going to get him talking to me, while you ran."

"But I wouldn't do that, Peter. It's just as much my fault as yours that we're in trouble. If you get caught, I won't leave you."

"You won't?" exclaimed Peter in surprise. He remembered how Bessie and his other London playmates rarely hesitated to desert a friend. Here was a new kind of girl, he thought—and a pretty good kind, too. He resolved to get her out of this scrape if he could. "Let's run for it," he said.

The short winter day was nearly over, and the gathering darkness outside made the children hope to slip past the house unseen. They would have succeeded, too, except that Captain Gallop remembered the barn door he had found open. "Can I be such a doddering old fool that I've left that door ajar again," he wondered. "I'll just have a look."

He stepped outside, and there stood two children right in his path! "Hey, what's this! What are you up to!" he growled.

Peter cast one desperate glance behind. No use! And the captain blocked the path ahead, so he started to plunge through the snow toward the road; but at that moment the magistrate, with two other men, came down the hill. Sally saw them, too. "Oh please, Captain Gallop," she cried, "don't let them get us."

"Come in here," said the captain gruffly. The children darted inside the house, and the captain slammed the door. "Now then, you've been in mischief; I can see that. What have you been doing?"

"We—we were up on Beacon Hill," began Sally. Then came a thundering knock on the door.

"Quick," said the captain, opening a cupboard. "In with you." The children did not need to be urged. They crawled into the closet which was just big enough to hold them, and there they crouched like two little rabbits in a hole. They heard the captain go to the door and talk to someone outside.

"Children in my house?" they heard him exclaim. "Are you crazy! You know I have neither wife nor child. I can't abide women, nor brats, neither.

"What's that you say? You saw two children come here! Well, step inside, and look for yourself! There's no one in this room but Tom Tucker. Maybe it was my cat you saw, Mr. Evans! There he sits by the fire. Does he look like two children to you, sir?"

There was a shuffling of feet as the three men crowded into the captain's little house. Someone laughed, and Evans, the magistrate, was heard indignantly denying that what he had seen was just the cat.

"Mr. Andrews—Mr. Johnson," the children heard the captain say, "does our good magistrate often see things this way? You haven't been having a go at the rum, have you, Mr. Evans? Now take my advice, sir, and give it up."

Once more poor Mr. Evans broke out in indignant protests. "There were two children, a boy and a girl, who got away. I gave chase, but I could not come close enough to see who they were!"

"Could someone tell me what Magistrate Evans is talking about?" interrupted Captain Gallop. "To me he seems confused. I have seen plenty of seamen in a state of—er—of confusion like this, and—"

"I never touch spirits," shouted the magistrate, goaded almost beyond endurance. "I tell you, a crowd of children have been sliding upon the snow on Beacon Hill. Their cries disturbed the peace, sir. Upon investigating, I found they had even taken benches from the new school house to use in their ungodly sport."

"What!" exclaimed Captain Gallop. "Such a thing could happen right under your nose and eyes, Magistrate! It's unbelievable! If I catch these limbs of Satan, I'll flog them well for you."

At last the children heard the front door close, and then their own door was flung open. They took a deep breath of air very gratefully, but they did not come out. "Come, come," said the captain. "Get up to the fire and warm yourselves. You're cold and wet."

Peter squared his shoulders. "I suppose you might as well whip me now, sir, and have done with it. But couldn't you let Sally go?"

"Come, come," said the captain, "get up to the fire and warm yourselves—you're cold and wet."

The captain looked puzzled for a minute, then he burst out laughing. "So you believe all you hear, do you, young man! You're as bad as poor old Evans."

When they were all gathered around the fire, the children told the captain their side of the story. "It was unseemly, I suppose, to take the benches," he chuckled. "But if I'd been there, I'd have joined in the sport.

"Now let me see. It's growing dark, Sally, and your mother will be worried. Take these eggs to her with my compliments; and if anyone should meet you on the road, they can see by your basket that you've been doing errands. Since the magistrate is looking for two children, you had best go by yourself."

Sally thanked Captain Webber. "I'll be careful not to break the eggs," she promised. "And I'll bring the basket back tomorrow." Her gray eyes were big and solemn, but when she looked at Peter, they were full of mischief. "Good-by—it was fun!" she said.

"And fun it must have been," chuckled Captain Gallop, as the door closed. "A lass of spirit, that's what she is. Well, my boy, wait a few minutes more. Then take this sixpence to the inn and get yourself some supper—that's my advice to you." He pulled out a strange-looking object, and handed it to Peter.

"Why, what is it, sir!" exclaimed Peter, turning the thing over in his hands. There were several white beads and a few dark purple ones sewed to a piece of leather.

"That's sixpence, I tell you," said Captain Gallop, enjoying Peter's bewilderment. "It's wampum—Indian money. It's just as good as the king's silver here in Boston, and I'll show you how to count it, so you won't be cheated. Six white beads are worth one penny, and three dark beads are worth the same."

65

"Can you really buy things with this, sir?" asked Peter, admiring the beautifully-rounded cylinders of shell.

"Cut along to the inn and see," laughed the captain. "To your left, then down the road. They've just put up a sign 'Cole's Inn.' It's the only one in town, so you can't miss it."

Peter found the inn readily enough. He pushed open the door and went inside, but for a moment he stood staring. Nothing looked as he expected. Instead of a noisy taproom with a bar, he saw a large, comfortable kitchen. A huge fire was burning on a hearth that took up the whole side of the room. A few people sat about, talking quietly. Peter thought he must have walked into someone's home uninvited, and he was about to go away again, when a pleasant-faced woman asked him to sit down. "The price of a meal is sixpence," she told him.

Peter, however, knew a good deal about innkeepers. "Can I have a whole meal for sixpence, or will there be extras?" he asked cautiously.

The woman smiled. "That magistrate over there would fine us ten shillings if I charged you more."

"Goodness," thought Peter, "magistrates everywhere!" He glanced quickly at the man indicated, and saw with relief that he was not the one who had been after him. "I'll have a meal then, ma'am." He handed the woman the piece of wampum, half expecting she would ask for silver instead, but she accepted it without comment. She went to a rack for a wooden plate, which she filled from a huge iron kettle hanging over the fire.

A boy entered, carrying a log of wood which he put on the hearth. Then he caught sight of Peter and came over to him, for he was one of the children who had been coasting on the hill. "Hello, Wunx," he said. "You got out of a good hiding!"

"William," said Mistress Cole sharply, " 'Satan finds some mischief still for idle hands to do.' Back to work, Will, before you get in trouble again."

"Now what was that he called me," wondered Peter. "Wunx! That doesn't sound like a good name to me."

Peter had nearly finished his meal when Captain Webber of the *Bachelor* came in, followed by Peter's new friend, Captain Gallop. "Rum!" bellowed Captain Webber, in his best quarter-deck voice. "Rum for two!"

Samuel Cole, the innkeeper, came hurrying over. "Quietly, gentlemen, quietly," he urged. "No rum sold here—dear me, of course not! Some beer? Some wine?"

"No rum?" exclaimed Captain Webber. "Who ever heard of such a thing! Well, bring wine, then: Madeira, if you have it."

Mr. Cole hurried away, and Captain Webber turned to his friend. "Do you mean to tell me I can't buy you a proper sailor's drink?" he demanded.

Captain Gallop chuckled. "The laws are very strict, and over there sits a magistrate. I don't say as you can't get rum—but now's a bad time to ask for it. At the top of your lungs, too! Poor old Cole is shaking in his shoes."

The Madeira arrived. "Your health, sir," said Captain Webber, raising his glass.

Captain Gallop laid a restraining hand on his friend's arm. "No, no," he whispered. "No healths—not even the king's. It's against the law."

Captain Webber drank his glass in silence, and called for another. "It's past me," he muttered "—all these laws."

Before he could order anything more, the magistrate appeared at his elbow. "It is my duty to inform you that you have

67

had enough," said this solemn-faced gentleman, indicating the empty glasses.

"Well I'll be—"

"Silence," said the man. "You are a stranger here, so it is now my duty to ask you a few questions. What is your business in Boston?"

"I'm sailing my ship *Bachelor* for 'The Company of Lords and Gentlemen'—but I don't see what business it is of yours."

"What is your religion?"

"Now this is too much!" roared Captain Webber, beginning to lose his temper. "My religion is my own affair. I fear God, and no man—do you hear? That's good enough for me, and it's going to be good enough for you, or by—"

"Be careful!" cried Captain Gallop, clapping a huge hand over his friend's mouth. "Blasphemy is against the law. You'll find yourself in the stocks if you don't watch out. Come on, Captain Webber. Let's go to my house—or your ship, if you've a mind. That's a fitter place for seafaring men."

"By the way, Gallop," the magistrate cut in. "Straighten that fence of yours at once. The court ordered you to line up those unsightly palings a month ago. You're liable to a fine, you know."

Captain Gallop's weather-beaten face turned a slightly darker shade of mahogany than usual, but he succeeded in holding his tongue.

Webber paid the score. Then he seemed to see Peter for the first time. "Come along with us, boy," he said. "This is no safe place for sailor men. I don't want to have to get you out of jail in the morning."

Peter fell in at a respectful distance behind the two captains.

It was quite dark now, and he was startled when a tall boy stepped out of a lane. He recognized the voice, however. "Hello, Wunx," said Sam anxiously. "Where's Sally?"

"She went home, carrying some eggs for her mother," said Peter, casually.

"Good old Wunx," chuckled Sam. "How did you do it! My shoulders are still sore from Evans' cane."

As the two boys walked down to the wharf, Peter told what had happened. "But why do you call me 'wunx,' Sam?" he asked. "Will called me that, too. What for? It doesn't sound good to me."

Sam laughed. "Why, you should be proud. That's the Indian name for fox, and we call you that because you got away from the magistrate so neatly. Now if we called you 'skunx,' that would be different." Sam held his nose significantly. "Wait till you meet one, that's all. Don't let anyone call you 'skunx,' but 'wunx' is a good name."

They reached the wharf. "Well, good-by," said Sam. He looked up at the *Bachelor*. Her hull lay dark against the water, but her masts and spars were touched with light from the rising moon. He sighed. "You're in luck to have such a good berth, Peter."

"She's a fine little ship," Peter agreed proudly. Then an idea struck him. "Would you really like a berth on her, Sam? Most of the sailors have left us to try their fortune in the New World. There's room for you, I know."

For a moment Sam listened joyfully. "I'll speak to the captain," he declared. Then he shook his head. "I'd have to get father's permission first," he said. "And I'm afraid father has other plans for me."

8: SAIL HO!

"NOVEMBER 28, 1635," Captain Webber had written in his log book the day the *Bachelor* arrived in Boston Harbor. Now the winter months rolled slowly by, and still the little ship lay at Long Wharf. Captain Webber was impatient to sail to Saybrook, discharge his cargo and begin his own trading expedition. "These 'Lords and Gentlemen' forsooth!" he would mutter, as he paced the deck. "My ship will rot at her moorings before they give me leave to go."

"What are we waiting for, sir?" Peter asked one day.

"We are waiting to carry out orders conceived in London by men who have never seen this wilderness," Captain Webber replied bitterly. "As I understand it, fifty carpenters were to have been sent to the Connecticut to erect houses suitable for gentlemen of quality. Of course, there are not fifty carpenters in America! Governor Winthrop managed to find twenty men who were willing to go—don't ask me how many of them are carpenters! Then came the early snow. If those twenty men managed to keep alive, they have done well. But they have been sent to build mansions and I suppose we will have to stay here till they do it. These precious 'Lords and Gentlemen' must have their fine city all prepared before they venture themselves!"

"The people of Boston were not like that," remarked Peter. "Sam's family lived in a dugout while they built their home."

"Of course," growled the captain. "But they are plain folk like you and me. Not titled gentlemen! But come now, shovel that snow off the after deck, and look sharp. I'll have no laziness aboard my ship, even if I do wait upon the whim of lords."

Sergeant Gardiner was no less impatient than Peter and the captain to be off for Saybrook. He and Mistress Gardiner were guests of the Winthrops, but they longed for a home of their own. "Do stay with us till a proper house is built for you in Saybrook," Mistress Winthrop urged. But Mary Gardiner declared that she would go to the Connecticut with her husband as soon as possible. She could live on board the boat, she explained. After that, a log cabin would do, at least for a while.

One day Peter borrowed the captain's brass telescope for a look at the shore. He soon saw that men with picks and shovels were assembling on one of Boston's "Three Mountains," as the hills were called. He promptly got shore leave, and went to see what was going on. He found old Job up there, in spite of his objections to going ashore in foreign ports. "We're building a fort for these Boston folk," he told Peter. "They've found out our Sergeant Gardiner is famous for forts in the Low Countries." Then he clapped his hand to his mouth. "There I go again," he exclaimed angrily. "Not 'Sergeant Gardiner' any more, Peter,

71

do you hear! It's 'Lieutenant' now. A proper little show of appreciation on the part of the governor. 'Lieutenant Gardiner' from now on—and I'd make him a general, if I stood in the governor's shoes. Yet I'm the one that cannot teach my tongue to use the new title."

Peter saw his friend approaching with maps and drawings in his hand. "Good morning, Lieutenant Gardiner," he said.

"Good morning, Seaman Cutler," said Lieutenant Gardiner, smiling, for Peter, too, had a new title. He was cabin boy no longer. Still more of the sailors had left the *Bachelor* now, and Peter had long since learned to sail the ship. He flushed with pleasure when Lieutenant Gardiner noticed his new dignity.

He wandered around in the snow on top of the hill for a while, expecting something exciting to happen. Job and the lieutenant squinted through strange instruments and shouted numbers. Surveying, they called it. Peter's feet got very cold, and he went back to the ship. He had begun to realize that there was more to building a fort than just raising a fine wall with a flag on top!

Sam came to see Peter whenever he could, but this was not often, for he worked hard. One day Captain Webber came on deck to find Peter showing Sam some rigging. He paused a moment, listening to the boys' talk. "So you like ships," he said to Sam. "Ever been to sea?"

"No, sir," Sam replied. "I went cod fishing, though, until last winter, so I know something about sailing. This year Master Parmount started up a school, and father makes me go."

"I take it you'd rather fish," said Captain Webber, smiling. "How old are you?"

"I'm fourteen, sir. I shall finish the long catechism and the

72

rule of three this winter. I hope that father will say I have schooling enough, then."

Peter could see that Captain Webber was looking at Sam's tall, strong figure with approval. "Sam can talk Indian language, sir," he put in, anxious to help his friend.

"That so!" exclaimed Captain Webber.

"Oh, I can make myself understood, all right," Sam replied modestly. "There are Narragansetts living not far from here, you know. A boy named Red Fox taught me to hunt with a bow and arrow."

"H'm, yes—a sensible thing to learn," commented Captain Webber. "Can you handle a gun?"

"I can shoot father's flintlock fairly well. He doesn't let me take it often, though, because powder and shot are costly."

"Have you ever thought of turning trader, instead of fisherman?"

"Indeed I have, sir." Sam's face brightened with eagerness. "I hear you are going trading, yourself, in the spring—and I'd like to join the venture. But—"

"But what?" asked Captain Webber impatiently. "I think you would do very well. I can offer you the same wages as Peter, here, and you can bring a stock to trade for yourself."

"But my father, sir," Sam explained. "I want nothing better than to go with you, but my father has plans for a journey westward in the spring. I must not say more. Where would you be going to trade, sir?"

"Why, up the Connecticut, I think."

"The Connecticut!" Sam's face brightened. "Oh then, sir, I'll tell that to my father—it might make a difference."

"Well, let me know soon," said the captain, "for I shall look

73

for someone else, if you cannot take the berth."

Sam promised, but days went by, and he sadly reported to Peter that his father had not yet consented.

It was January 23, 1636, according to Captain Webber's log, when Lieutenant Gardiner came on board the *Bachelor,* one bitter cold morning. "Can we be off to Saybrook?" wondered Peter. He was disappointed not to see Mistress Gardiner as well. "It is too cold for her," he supposed. He knew better than to ask questions, but sprang up the icy ropes into the rigging to unfurl the sail.

Before long Peter's questions were answered. The little ship took a northerly course toward Salem. "It's the Town of Salem wants a fort now," said William Job, as the *Bachelor* sailed up Massachusetts Bay. "Lieutenant Gardiner can make his fortune, if he will. These towns, it seems, are in fear of the French. They all want forts, and will pay, somehow, to get them."

But in a day or two the *Bachelor* was once more bound for Boston. "Is there to be no fort at Salem, sir?" Peter ventured to ask the lieutenant.

"No," his friend replied. "I never saw a town better fortified by nature. But the townspeople are poor. I told them, 'First, conquer Captain Hunger. Spend money for food, and then, after a good harvest, there will be time enough to build a fort, if one be needed.' "

"But what about the French?" asked Peter.

"Listen," said Lieutenant Gardiner. "War is like a three foot stool. Want one leg, and down comes all. Now these three legs are men, victuals and munitions. Do you understand, Peter? We and the French are all fighting Captain Hunger together, here in America—at least for a time."

74

Peter thought he understood fairly well what the lieutenant meant. Of one thing he was sure, however—his lieutenant was a great man. He would not make a fortune—and cause unnecessary suffering by building forts people didn't need.

Once more the *Bachelor* was tied up in Boston. The fort on the hill had taken shape. Peter often went there to see it. At last, February, with its short, dreary days, was gone, and it was March, with its piercing winds. "Does spring never come in America?" Peter asked Sam one morning.

"When the days begin to lengthen, the cold begins to strengthen," Sam replied. "Father has all sorts of rhymes for weather, and that's the one he's always telling us now. But there is a spring—you wait and see."

"Wait!" exclaimed Peter. "That's all I ever do!"

Peter's waiting was more nearly over than he or Sam guessed, however. Up at the Winthrop house, Mistress Gardiner and Eliza were busily packing boxes. Lieutenant Gardiner and John Winthrop the younger were having a last conference about the affairs of the Company of Lords and Gentlemen. Lieutenant Gardiner was commander of the fort, but Winthrop was governor of the future colony at Saybrook. "I shall wait here, then, for news from England," said Winthrop. "The *True Love* is long over-due. She should come in soon with the rest of our supplies, with colonists for Saybrook, perhaps, and money."

The very next day Sam came dashing down the hill to the wharf. He was nearly bursting with good news, for his father had at last consented to let him go trading. When he reached the water-side, however, he stopped abruptly—the *Bachelor* was gone!

For a moment, Sam had the wild idea that she must have

sunk, and he peered into the icy water. There was nothing, of course. The March wind howled dismally in the rigging of the *Rebecca*, tied up close by. There was no other sound. Sam stared at the empty space along the wharf. Could they have gone trading without him? No, because the Indians were still in the north. Trade could not start till the tribes came back to the coast, bringing their furs.

"Hey, mate." A voice from the *Rebecca* made Sam spin around. A tanned and rather tarry old seaman was peering over the rail at him. "Be you Sam West? Be you looking for a likely lad named Peter?"

Sam nodded. "Then I was to tell you as he'd sailed for Saybrook on the turn of the tide. 'Back by spring,' he says. He's going to fix it up for ye with the captain, if he can—whatever that means." Whereupon the old sailor spat overside once, then shuffled off about his business.

"Good old Peter," thought Sam. "He can fix it up for me, if anyone can!"

Sam stood on the wharf, gazing longingly out to sea. He hoped to catch a glimpse of the *Bachelor*, but she had set out with a fair wind, and was now heeling over, and scudding along out of sight of land. There was something on the horizon, though! A tiny white cloud? No, a sail, for certain.

"Sail ho! Sail ho!" cried Sam excitedly. For months, no ship had made Boston Harbor. There had been no news from the Old World, and those people who had families and friends in England had begun to feel as if they lived on another planet.

"Where away?" called the old sailor on the *Rebecca*. Sam pointed, and ran home to tell the news. But he need not have hurried. It was many hours before the *True Love* of London docked in Boston. By that time the whole town had assembled.

Among the passengers, Sam noticed a tall man, somewhat stooped, with graying hair. No friends came forward to greet him; yet, he seemed to be searching for someone. Perhaps he felt Sam's friendly interest, for he approached the boy. "Is there a ship called *'Bachelor'* in port here?" he asked.

"There was, until this morning," Sam replied. "She sailed with the turn of the tide."

"Sailed!" gasped the man. "Not—not back to England?"

"Oh, no. She's gone to the Connecticut."

The man sighed wearily. "I suppose you could not tell me if there was a lad named Peter Cutler aboard?"

"Indeed there was. He's a friend of mine."

"Then which way to this Connecticut? There are no coaches, I suppose, but where can I hire a horse?"

Sam politely concealed a smile, though he had a great desire to laugh, as he pictured an English mail coach attempting the forest trails. "There is no road, sir," he said, "let alone a coach. The Connecticut trail is very rough, and it is a hundred miles long. There are deep rivers to ford, and the way is not well marked in places."

It was plain that the stranger was astonished. "Everyone said this New World was big," he exclaimed, "but I had no idea the Connecticut would be so far away. I suppose I will pass through towns where I may rest, on the way?"

Sam shook his head. "The trail leads right through the forest. The savages made it long ago."

"Well," said the man, "I have come too long a distance to give up now. I will reach the Connecticut somehow, if that is where my son has gone."

77

Sam came dashing down the hill to the wharf—

—the "Bachelor" was gone!

"Your son!" exclaimed Sam. "Peter never told me he was expecting his father."

Mr. Cutler smiled. "He could not have told you about me. My boy supposed I was dead."

When Mr. Cutler told Sam a little about how he had lost his family and how he was searching for Peter, Sam wished he had not made the way to the Connecticut seem so hard. "You will find each other soon, I'm sure," he declared "—and how happy Peter will be!"

"First, I have letters for the Winthrops, which I must deliver before I continue my journey," said Mr. Cutler. "Could you direct me to the house?"

Sam walked to the Winthrops' with Mr. Cutler, answering many eager questions on the way. Later in the day he found Mr. Cutler again—this time at Cole's Inn. "My mother bids you stay with us, sir," he said. "That is, unless you have other friends in Boston."

Peter's father found a warm welcome at the Wests'. But when they heard he meant to start for the Connecticut at once, they tried to dissuade him. "At least, wait until a company of people are setting out," said Sam's father. " 'Tis far safer."

"Mr. Winthrop has kindly offered to lend me a horse, if I will carry letters to Lieutenant Gardiner," said Mr. Cutler. "It is an offer I cannot afford to refuse. And even if it were not for that, my own impatience would speed me on to find my boy."

So, after spending only a few days in Boston, Robert Cutler set out alone. The Wests said good-by to him with many misgivings. They drew him a rude map, and told him all they knew about the trail. But Robert Cutler had no experience in the wilderness. He lost the trail after traveling three days!

9: THE FORT ON THE RIVER

AS for Peter, he was happy to be at sea again after so many months of waiting. It was rough and stormy off Cape Cod, but at last the storm blew itself out.

There came a clear, cold morning, when Peter saw the broad Connecticut for the first time. "But this is no river," he cried, rubbing his eyes. "This is like a great bay. It's not brown, like the Thames; it's as blue as the sea!" The little ship drew closer to the shore, and on the western bank, Peter saw red sandstone cliffs.

The Gardiners came hurrying on deck. "Saybrook! Saybrook!" they said to each other. It was hard to believe. But now they could make out a sort of framework on top of the cliff. There was something bright mounted on it, reflecting the sun.

"The captain's compliments, and here is a telescope for you, lieutenant," said Peter. He was careful to use his friend's new and higher title. "Not Sergeant now—Lieutenant Gardiner," Peter reminded himself.

Lieutenant Gardiner focused the brass telescope on the rude framework at the cliff's head. "My fort!" he cried, laughing, and handed the glass to his wife. "Look, they have even mounted one brass cannon!"

"But—but the portcullis—the drawbridge," stammered Peter. "This river is so big, you cannot use the drawbridge that we have on board."

Lieutenant Gardiner laughed again. "Who cares, lad! With a river like this, we don't need a drawbridge. Oh, what a country! Forget about drawbridges—they're for old lands with little rivers. This is all big and new and different. We'll melt the iron down, and hammer it into something useful—shovels—plows, mayhap. Why, with a cliff and a great river, I need but a palisade, such as the Indians build. Then a brass cannon or two—and I'll make Saybrook safe for Lords and Gentlemen. And even ladies," he added, looking at his wife's happy face.

Peter did not know whether to be disappointed or glad, because Saybrook was so different from everything he had imagined. His visions of a tall stone castle with himself, perhaps, as warder, letting down the drawbridge, began to fade like a childish dream. He saw that many of the ideas he had brought over with him from the Old World were to be of no use in the New. He looked about him; at the great river sweeping down out of the wilderness; at the forest stretching away as far as eye could reach, and he felt very small and rather lonely. On top of the cliff, a puff of smoke caught his eye. A few seconds later came the boom of the little cannon.

A few seconds later came the boom of the little cannon.

"They're saluting us," shouted Peter. His mood of loneliness left him instantly. He was now part of a gallant venture, and he knew it.

When the *Bachelor* tied up on shore, Sergeant Willard, who was in charge at Saybrook, assembled his twenty men to greet their new commander. They were a sorry-looking lot. Provisions had given out, and they had been living on nuts and roots. They had frozen their feet trying to catch fish through the ice. Game was impossible to find in the snow. Lieutenant Gardiner took one look at them. "Break out our stores," he said to Willard. "Set cook fires going. The first thing to do is to give these men of yours a good meal."

A cheer went up from the ragged ranks. Lieutenant Gardiner was already a popular commander.

"The fort won't look like much to you, sir," said Sergeant Willard, as Gardiner climbed the ladder to the platform and stood beside the gun. "It's proved useful, though. We no sooner had this cannon heaved up here" (he patted the little piece affectionately) "than one of our men sighted a Dutch sloop. She'd come to take possession of this point, sir, without a doubt. Thinks I, it's no use letting her come close enough to see we've no proper fort and no force of men, to speak of. We let off our cannon. Well sir, that sloop just came about, and sailed away again. She never even fired a shot."

"Splendid," laughed Lieutenant Gardiner. "Let us hope all our engagements are as easily won. But now, sergeant, you are dismissed to get some food for yourself. Judging by your 'lean and hungry look,' you have fared no better than your men."

Lieutenant Gardiner seated himself on the rough scaffolding

that was some day to become a fort. Below, a little to the west, lay trees which had been felled, and were lying where they had fallen. Some of their branches had been lopped off—some not. Here and there a ring of melted snow showed where the men had been burning brush.

Peter, who had been exploring the clearing, now came scrambling up the ladder to look at the gun. He saw that Lieutenant Gardiner had a paper spread out upon his knee. "Plan of ye City of Sayebrook" were the words printed across the top, with many a flourish.

"Do you see that big mud hole yonder?" asked Gardiner, his eyes twinkling. "That is called on the map 'a generous square'; and look at that bark shack that resembles a dog kennel. You can tell by a glance at the plan, Peter, that it is one of the 'houses for gentlemen of figure and distinction.' "

As Peter looked at the hut in question, a man came crawling out on hands and knees. The door was too low to permit him to stand upright. Peter laughed. "Can't you just see Mr. Fenwick in his red velvet cloak, crawling out of that hole!"

Lieutenant Gardiner laughed, too, but then his face grew serious. "Just wait, my boy; there'll be houses for gentlemen of distinction in Saybrook. Who knows—one of them might belong to Peter Cutler, Esquire, some day! Now run to the boat and get Mr. Job."

"Yes, sir," said Peter, darting off.

"You will have to go ashore now, Mr. Job," he said, when he found the man. "Aren't you afraid of savages?"

"That I be," said Job with a sigh, "but duty is duty. If Lieutenant sends for me, I go."

Peter laughed at poor old Job's fears, but if he could have had a magic glimpse into the future, he would not have laughed at all!

The sandstone cliffs of Saybrook which Lieutenant Gardiner had admired so much proved a great difficulty in the matter of unloading cargo. "I could stand off an army here with a handful of men," he declared. "Alas, I can also stand off my own supplies!"

Peter turned himself into a regular little pack pony, as he climbed the steep cliff again and again, carrying as heavy loads as he was able. In spite of everyone's best efforts, however, the work, which should have been accomplished in a few days, dragged on for weeks.

One morning, while Peter climbed the path, he heard a sweet, clear whistle. He stopped short and listened, for the sound was unlike anything he had ever heard before. There it came again, and Peter saw a bird with a back as blue as the sky. It flew into a thicket of small trees, whose shoots had begun to turn a beautiful red. There Peter saw a whole flock of bluebirds darting about, showing flashes of living color in their swooping flight. Peter felt a strange lifting of heart. The cold winds still blew; the trees were still bare, but he knew that it was spring.

The great river grew swollen and angry, flooded with melting snows from the north. And at last, one morning the *Bachelor* sailed out with a boiling tide. It was well she did, for the Connecticut was fighting hard to drive her far out into the Sound, and she could hardly be held at her moorings.

10: A WARNING

THE *Bachelor* reached Boston after a hard trip around Cape Cod. And there, on Long Wharf, was Sam, waving his cap and shouting a greeting. "Father says I can go trading," he called to Peter, as he helped tie up the boat.

The arrangements with Captain Webber were quickly made. Now, it was Seaman West of the *Bachelor,* and Peter clapped his friend on the back.

The captain and the two boys went together to the shops along the waterfront to buy trade goods for their venture. "By the way," said Sam, as they walked along, "you must have had a fine surprise at Saybrook. Didn't someone come there to see you?"

"No," said Peter. "Why?"

Sam's face fell. They were at the door of a shop; there was

no time to talk. "Never mind," he said. "I'll tell you about it later."

Mr. West, having finally decided to make a trader of his son, had given him a few pieces of silver and a string or two of wampum. It was all and more than the family could afford. Sam and Peter bought some blue cloth and some red. "The Indian women always choose blue," said Sam.

"We'll need more red then," said Peter. "From what you have told me about Indians, the women do most of the work, and it is the men who have the time to dress themselves up and paint their faces!"

A shadow darkened the door of the little shop, and Sam turned to see a young Indian lad of about his own age enter. "Why, Red Fox!" he cried. "When did you come back from the north?"

"Me come on flood water down river this morning," said Red Fox, shaking hands a little stiffly. He had passed the whole winter in the North Woods, where he had grown to be all Indian, forgetting about the white settlers' ways.

Sam, too, had changed. He had been in school, where Indian wisdom would not have been tolerated. "How was the hunting?" he asked, trying to put his friend at his ease.

"You come see," said Red Fox. "Me got two, three pretty fine pelts. Me show you. You come to our village? Hunt with Red Fox again?"

"I'll come to your village, all right," Sam declared. "But I can't hunt with you this summer. I'm going to be a trader."

Red Fox scowled. "No, no," he exclaimed. "You no trader. Trader cheat. You friend. You hunt with me."

"But I am your friend, and I won't cheat you or your people,

Red Fox. You want to sell your furs, you know. Look at this cloth. See these beads? Don't you want me to come in a ship and bring your people many things like this?"

Red Fox thought for a while in silence. The shopkeeper had articles laid out temptingly—but out of reach. He looked them all over. "Very good," he said at last. "When you come, I show you to my people. I say, 'This boy my friend. No cheat.' My people bring out best furs to trade—you see!"

"Good," cried Sam. "It's a bargain. Let's shake hands on it. Now look around, Red Fox, and tell me what you see that you think your people would like best."

"Here is something the French use," said the shopkeeper. "They get a great heap of furs for a very little of this cinnabar."

"Cinnabar?" questioned Peter. "What is it?"

The shopkeeper took a small amount of red powder, moistened it, and drew his finger across his cheek. There appeared a bright red mark.

"Red paint," exclaimed Peter, still puzzled. "What's the use of that?"

But Red Fox's face showed as much eagerness as his Indian dignity would permit. "Yes, yes, bring fine war paint!" he exclaimed. "No berry in the forest make red mark so fine like that."

"We have verdigrease, too," said the shopkeeper, and he demonstrated the green paint as well.

Red Fox's eyes glistened. "That very fine paint, too."

"And mirrors," suggested the shopkeeper, "so the braves can see their fine paint."

Red Fox examined the tiny looking-glass with such solemn attention that Peter had to try not to laugh. "I know the magic stone," the Indian boy said gravely. "Chiefs have them."

"And I will give you one for your own, Red Fox," said Sam, "when I come to trade. You tell your friends to keep all their best furs for us, and you shall have a mirror just like a chief."

"That's a good stroke of business, boy," said Captain Webber, when Red Fox had gone. "You seem to have a knack for getting along with Redskins, Sam."

Peter, seeing the Captain in such a good mood, promptly asked for shore leave—and got it. He had been invited to Sam's house to spend the night. "What would it feel like," he wondered, "to sleep in a real bed?"

As Peter and Sam set out upon the road, Peter noticed that Sam seemed to have something on his mind. "Well, I've told you all about Saybrook," he said. "Now what have you been doing?"

"Oh school," said Sam. "Master Parmount's birch rod for most of us."

"Is that all?" said Peter, disappointed.

"Well, we had a visitor a while ago."

Peter waited, but Sam did not go on till Peter asked what visitor.

"All right," said Sam laughing. "I'll tell you now. I was going to wait till we got home, but the news is too good to keep any longer. Peter, your father visited us. He has come to America to find you."

Peter stopped stock still in the road, and stared at Sam. "Who? My father! What do you mean!"

"Oh, Peter!" cried Sam, "I forgot you thought he was dead. I should have let mother break the news gently, as she calls it."

Peter laughed. "I'm glad you didn't. Only please go on and

90

tell me more. I still don't understand how my father could be here, when everyone told me he died in prison."

"He escaped, Peter. He told us he was in Newgate many years. He gave up hope of ever getting free, when a new turnkey came who proved to be a Puritan, like himself. Together they arranged that your father should disappear one night, and a new prisoner take his place."

"Oh," said Peter, remembering what Mr. Hopkins had told him in London. "That must be the jailer who told a friend of mine that my father was surely dead. The inquiries must have frightened the poor turnkey considerably. But tell me quickly, Sam—where is my father now?"

"He's gone to find you. We told him you were at Saybrook, of course, so he took horse and set out along the trail. I wonder that you did not see him at the fort, before you left!"

Peter's heart sank like lead. "Oh where can my father be!" he cried. "No one came looking for me at Saybrook."

Sam was by this time alarmed about Mr. Cutler, but he tried to conceal his fears from Peter. "Now don't look so downhearted," he protested. "Five minutes ago you did not think you had a father at all. Now you not only have a father, but you're bound to find him soon. Any one of a number of things could have happened to delay his trip. Perhaps his horse went lame. Maybe the streams were flooded, and he had to wait for lower water."

They had reached Sam's house by this time. Sam's mother was stirring a great iron pot that hung over the fireplace, when the boys arrived. She turned to greet them, and her smiling gray eyes were just like Sally's. And there was little Sally, herself, drawing a high-backed settle into the middle of the room; then, to Peter's surprise, she turned the back down to make a table. She smiled shyly at Peter.

"Have you been hiding in the hay lately?" asked Peter.

Sally blushed, but then she forgot her shyness and began to laugh. "I only hunt for hen's eggs," she said demurely, with a cautious glance at her elders.

Peter helped her fasten the table top in place by means of wooden pegs. He thought it was a very clever piece of furniture—now a seat, now a table—whenever you please. "We have such a small house," Sally explained, "that almost everything in it must do double duty. We shall have a much better house, I hope, when we get to the—" She clapped her hand over her mouth, and looked anxiously at her mother. "Never mind where, Peter," she added, " 'twas something I am not supposed to tell."

"Idle tongues always make mischief, Sara," said her mother. "Now set about your work with more diligence and less chatter. Peter might like to go to the barn to help Sam with his chores."

Peter took the hint, and departed. He found Sam milking the cow, while one of his brothers split wood and the other pitched down hay to feed the horse. "Hello, Wunx," said Sam. "Do you like to milk?"

"I don't know," Peter replied. "I never tried it, but it looks easy."

Nathan, Sam's oldest brother, laughed. "Let him try," he suggested.

Peter sat down on the little three-legged stool, and tried to do just as he had seen Sam doing. The results, however, were not the same. The cow slashed him in the face with her tail, and nearly kicked over the bucket. "Look out!" exclaimed

Nate, "if we spill that milk, there'll be trouble."

"Trouble and dry corn meal mush for supper, as well," laughed Sam. "Give me back the bucket, Peter."

Peter felt very foolish. He tried to help Nathan split firewood, but he was awkward with the axe.

Sally came running out to the barn, a cloak pulled hastily around her shoulders. "Mother says to hurry, boys. Oh Peter, look out! You'll cut yourself. Better let Nate split the wood; he works faster."

Poor Peter! How he wished there was something about a farm that he could do. "You'd never suppose my father was a farmer," he thought. Just then a furious barking broke out. The children ran to the door to see Pollux, their big black dog, standing on the well curb, barking loudly. "Here, Pollux, come here," called Sam. The dog came, but went right back to the

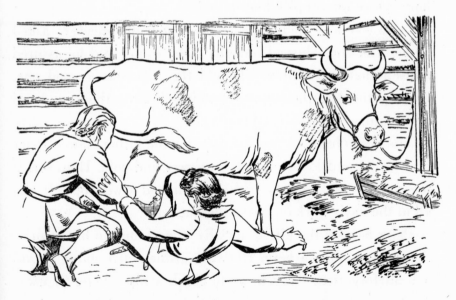

**The cow slashed him in the face with her tail,
and nearly kicked over the bucket.**

well again.

The children followed him this time, and looked down the well. It was dark down there, but they could make out something white struggling in the water. "It's my kitten," exclaimed Sally. "Oh, she'll drown. Oh, how could she have fallen in! What shall I do!"

The West children looked at each other helplessly, but Peter was examining the strong rope that was wrapped around a wooden drum across the top of the well. "How does this thing work?" he asked.

This time no one thought of laughing at him for his ignorance of settlers' ways. The boys turned the handle, and showed him how the rope was fastened to a bucket, which was lowered into the well. "But look at the silly kitten," cried Sally, almost in tears. "She won't try to climb into the bucket; she'll drown long before we can pick her up in it."

"Can you hold the handle, so the rope hangs steady?" asked Peter. The boys showed him that they could, and he assured himself that the knot which held the rope was a good one. Then, without further ado, he let himself down the rope, hand over hand.

The climb back was not so easy, for the kitten clawed Peter frantically, and Peter's hands were wet and cold. However, it was not the first time he had ever climbed a wet rope. It was all in the day's work on board the *Bachelor*.

Peter handed the kitten to Sally, then found to his surprise that he was quite a hero. His awkwardness at evening chores was all forgotten. "Teach me to climb a rope, Peter?" asked Nathan.

"Oh, it's nothing. Certainly I will," said Peter, grinning.

The children all gathered around the supper table, where at first they sat with bowed heads while Sam's father prayed at considerable length. "I wish grown-ups got as hungry as children do," thought Peter with a sigh.

After the blessing, Sally started to tell her mother about the rescue of the kitten, but her mother shook her head. "Children should be seen and not heard at table, Sara."

Peter, who had been about to speak, hastily shut his mouth again. "What part of England do you come from, Peter?" asked Mr. West.

Peter looked down at his plate. "Speak when you are spoken to," said Mistress West.

"From London, sir," Peter replied promptly. ("They have a rule for everything," he thought.)

Mr. West looked a little annoyed. "Yes, yes—we most of us sail from London. I mean before that."

"Well—I used to live in Amesbury once," said Peter.

To his surprise, this answer seemed to please his host. Sam's father and mother exchanged glances, and then the questions continued. "You have relatives, I suppose?"

"Yes," said Peter, "Sam has just told me I have a father who is looking for me!" Peter's dark eyes shone like stars when he said this, and everyone at the table smiled in sympathy, although Sam's father looked a little reproachfully at his son.

"Girls are not alone in their love of gossip, it seems," remarked Mr. West. "But surely your father found you at Saybrook, Peter."

"No," said Peter, the light dying out of his eyes. "He did not come."

Mr. West exchanged a quick glance of consternation with his

wife. "Ah well, he is there by now," he said, but his tone lacked conviction.

"Do you remember your father, Peter?" asked Mistress West.

Peter shook his head. "I try to, but I can't," he said. "He was a tall man with brown hair. He used to put me on his shoulder."

"His hair is gray, now," said Mistress West. "Have you anything—any little thing you kept, that belonged to your family? Sam told your father how you look now, but he longs for some sign to show that you are really his son."

"I have one thing," said Peter. "It is my mother's miniature. But I left it at Saybrook, in Mistress Gardiner's care."

"That was wise," approved Mistress West. "Perhaps we are all of us destined to meet on the Connecticut. If Peter will be careful not to gossip, shall we tell him where next he may find us?"

Her husband assented. "It may be hard for you to understand, Peter. But we seek a thing we call 'religious freedom.' It means the right to think and speak as we please about the Bible. We feel we must leave Boston."

Peter considered for a moment. He remembered his own difficulties upon his first day ashore in Boston. "Are there too many magistrates?"

Sam's father's serious expression relaxed a trifle. "Exactly," he said. "So, very soon, we shall all go to the Connecticut."

As Mr. West spoke these words, a sudden draft made the candles flicker, and the family turned, startled, to stare at the door, which had opened silently.

"No go!" came a voice from the outer darkness. "Friends of Red Fox, no go Quon-ec-ti-cut!"

II: TRADING

THE solemn tones of Red Fox's warning sent chills down Peter's spine. He gazed, fascinated, at the slowly opening door. Mr. West jumped up and reached for the long fowling piece that hung on the wall. No one else moved.

Red Fox entered the room with his right hand upraised, however, to show that he came as a friend, without weapons. Mr. West sat down again with a sigh of relief. His wife broke the tense silence.

"What does your Indian friend mean by spying on us like this, Sam? He was listening at our door!"

"Oh Mother, that's just his way," Sam explained. "He's been taught to creep up silently, and he thinks it's only common sense to listen awhile, before he appears. He doesn't understand that we call that bad manners. Can't I ask him to sit down and tell us what his warning means?"

"Very well," sighed Mistress West. "Trust an Indian to appear at mealtimes. Get me another plate, Sally. He is hungry, I suppose. They all are." Peter noticed that she filled the pewter plate generously for Sam's Indian friend, although she evidently did not approve of him.

Red Fox declined a chair, preferring to sit on the floor, but he accepted the plate with a grunt of satisfaction. For a while there was nothing to be heard except the Indian enjoying his food. Then he began to speak. To Peter's disappointment, Red Fox spoke in his own tongue, but Sam seemed able to understand. The Indian accompanied his talk with gestures, and as the story grew more intense, even Peter could follow it to a certain extent. He heard the word "English," then he saw Red Fox draw a hand across his throat and make a choking noise. "No mistaking that," thought Peter. "Somebody plans to kill the English!" He heard the name "Pequot," and again there was a vivid pantomime of war to accompany Red Fox's words. "So it's Pequots—whoever they may be," thought Peter. "They are the ones who are after us." The Indian put his now empty plate upon the floor.

He rose, and looked about him. "Friends of Red Fox," he repeated in English, "No go Quon-ec-ti-cut." Then he left the house without another word.

"Well, Sam, tell us what he says," Mr. West commanded. "What does he mean by this 'No go Connecticut' nonsense?"

"And leave the door open a minute, Sam," Mistress West put in. "I can't stand that smell of bear's grease your friend left behind him!"

"Red Fox says the Connecticut country is bad medicine," Sam began. "Of course, I couldn't understand every word, but

I know this: a tribe of Indians called 'Pequots' are living there, and Red Fox thinks they mean mischief. He has been hearing tales around the camp fire all winter. First, the Pequots came from the West, and they conquered Red Fox's people. That was many moons ago. Now they are boasting that they will drive out the white men, too, but they want the Narragansetts to help them. They propose that the Narragansetts surround Boston some night—burn and kill! They promise to serve the Dutch and English on the Connecticut the same way."

"Ridiculous!" exclaimed Sam's father. "The Indians will never rise against us."

"That's what I think, Father. They like to trade with us too well to fight us. But Red Fox says these Pequots are different."

"Very well, suppose they are indeed 'a horse of another color.' They cannot hurt us. Of what use are stone arrowheads against a British breast-plate!"

"But the Pequots have guns, Father. Red Fox says that they boast they have killed two traders. They show their scalps at the council fire, and declare they have taken guns, as well."

"It is true—the traders, Stone and Norton, were killed on the Connecticut," said Sam's father. "It was in the summer of 1634, I think, and there was talk of punishing the savages for it, but nothing was done."

"Red Fox says the Narragansetts hate and distrust the Pequots. They will not join them against us—at least for the present. But he insists that we must not trust ourselves alone among the Pequots, for fear they will kill us—if only to impress the other tribes."

"I think you have a true friend in Red Fox," said Mr. West, slowly. "Doubtless he believes we will be in danger. But after fasting and prayer, I have made my decision, and I shall not change it. We remove westward in June, at the latest."

Sam knew better than to say any more to his father. Later, after he and Peter had climbed the ladder into the loft, they whispered together before they went to sleep.

"Do you believe what Red Fox says, Sam?"

"Yes. He is my friend—he wouldn't lie."

Peter sighed. "Then I wish my father hadn't gone to the Connecticut. Are you sure he is really my father, Sam?"

"Who?" asked Sam, almost asleep. "Oh, Mr. Robert Cutler? Yes, Peter, I'm sure. You know, somehow he made me think of you."

Sam dropped off to sleep, but Peter lay awake listening to the wind. He thought of his father, somewhere in this vast new world. "Suppose the Pequots have killed him," he thought. "Suppose he is lost in the forest. Oh what shall I do!" He heard a terrifying cracking sound—then a thud, as the wind brought down a branch from a nearby tree. "What a blow we're having! A northeaster. I'm glad I'm not rounding Cape Cod tonight. I'll wager Captain Webber is looking to our mooring ropes, even though we are safe in port."

But next morning, Peter discovered that a boat is not necessarily safe while in port. The *Bachelor* had broken loose during the night, and nothing but Captain Webber's fine seamanship kept her from piling up on the rocks. He had managed to beach her on a small spit of sand, but she had three planks stove in near the bow.

Peter found the little barque on shore near the Charles River, where some obliging settlers were helping to pull her out of reach of the tide. They had cut some small trees to make rollers, but the work was slow. "She can be repaired right where she is, and then launched again," declared Captain Webber. "But repaired with what! Aye, there's the difficulty. We must needs use green lumber. Bound to swell or shrink with every change in the weather!"

"True," agreed Captain Gallop, who had come to "bear a hand," as he said. "Not only will your wood be green, but where will you get planks? Why, you must first find you a good sawyer and two helpers. They fell your tree. They dig a saw pit. Then, they rip the log lengthwise with their big two-man saw. It's slow work, and skillful work. You'll not find it easy to get a good sawyer."

Captain Webber groaned. His friend was not encouraging, to put it mildly. "And what about my trading venture?" he complained. "I have bought my goods. The Indians will sell their furs to other traders, while I stick here in the mud. I shall be ruined."

Captain Gallop nodded. He was watching a little vessel beating her way down the river. "There goes Captain Oldham's pinnace, now," he said. "She's bound for the Connecticut, and she'll be loaded with prime beaver skins before any of us." He paused and cleared his throat. "I hate to see a friend aground like this," he continued somewhat hesitantly. "There's one thing you could do, if you've a mind. You could put your goods aboard my barque. I plan to go out any day now, you know. You could send your lad Peter along to keep an eye on your interests."

Captain Webber swung around, a broad smile on his weather-beaten face. "You say, if I've a mind!" he exclaimed. "Why Cap'n, you're a life-saver, man. My interests, indeed! I know an honest man when I see one, I hope! But you can have the boy Peter, for he's a good seaman." The two captains shook hands on the bargain.

"By the way," said Captain Gallop, "I hear you've taken on the Wests' youngest son. Do you want him now? I would engage him myself, and the three of us could handle my barque nicely."

Peter was overjoyed to hear Captain Webber agree to the transfer of Sam, also. He was dispatched to find Sam at once, tell him the news and set to work loading Captain Gallop's barque. Before night, a slightly bewildered but happy Peter was sailing out of Boston harbor. "Bound for the Connecticut," thought Peter. "Surely I shall find my father soon."

At the last moment, Sally had come running down to the wharf with a big copper kettle. "Mother says she can spare it," the little girl declared breathlessly, "but oh! Sam, do get plenty of furs for it, so we can buy at least two more. I don't really know how we shall cook our food till you get back."

Sam promised. "The Indians will give a lot for a copper kettle," he explained to the rather puzzled Peter. "You see, they need kettles to boil the sap from the sugar maples. Their own buckets are made of bark, which cannot stand the heat. With a copper kettle, you can make maple sugar, which the Indians love dearly. So do I," he added, grinning.

"Good-by, Sally. I'll strike a good bargain, never fear." What had seemed to Sam like just a boy's adventure suddenly became much more serious. He realized that he had been entrusted with an important share of the family fortune.

"Good-by, Peter," said Sally. "Mother said I might give you these hose. I knitted them myself."

"Just like Sam's!" exclaimed Peter with delight. He was so pleased and surprised that he hardly knew how to say "thank you." "This is what it feels like to have a family," he thought. The last thing he saw in the little town of Boston he had come to love was the tiny, distant figure of Sally, standing on the wharf, waving a kerchief.

But now the joy of the open sea claimed both the boys. They looked forward, not back. Their adventure had begun. By morning, they were sailing up Narragansett Bay, blue and beautiful, dotted with islands and seemingly stretching away for miles.

Red Fox's village was soon reached, and when Sam made himself known, the tribe brought out their choicest furs. "We

Red Fox's village was soon reached.

no got many," Red Fox explained sadly. "Pequots take best hunting grounds." Those Indians who understood his words nodded and scowled.

"H'm," said Captain Gallop to the boys, "sounds like we'd better set sail for the Pequot River then, when we've done here."

"No, no!" exclaimed Red Fox, who overheard him. "No go!"

"He always says that," Sam explained. Sam was beginning to think his friend's warning was rather a joke. In that, however, he was never more mistaken in his life.

Next day Captain Gallop decided that there were indeed few furs to be had among the Narragansetts. The Pequot River flowed into the sound an easy day's sail to the west, and he set out accordingly. Threatening clouds were rolling up in the east. The old sea captain cocked a weather-wise eye at them, and decided he could make the river mouth before the storm.

He was wrong. The wind rose, and soon the little barque was scudding along before a gale. "Just so we keep her off the rocks, boys," he bellowed above the storm. "That's the main thing. Never mind where we be, exactly. We'll make the Pequot River sometime—but not tonight, I reckon."

When morning dawned, the storm had blown itself out, but the Pequot River was miles away. "There's Block Island," said Captain Gallop, pointing at the land ahead. "Well, there are Indians there, too. We'll just try our luck, since we're here."

The barque drew closer to the shore. "A ship on our port bow, sir," said Peter.

"Aye, to be sure," said Captain Gallop, "and by the cut of her jib, she's Captain Oldham's boat. Now, has he left us anything worth trading for, I wonder."

They drew nearer. "Why, the deck is swarming with Indians," exclaimed Sam. "That's queer."

"It is mighty queer, lad," said Captain Gallop. "Take the tiller, Peter, while I go forward to have a look. See that! The savages have spied our boat, and some of them are jumping into canoes and paddling away like mad.

"Mighty queer. Mighty queer." Peter saw that Captain Gallop's face had become grim and tense. They were fairly close, now.

"Oldham," bellowed Captain Gallop, cupping his hands. "John Oldham, ahoy! Is all well?"

There was no answer.

12 : THE SEA FIGHT

"LOOK, look!" shouted Peter, pointing excitedly at the pinnace. "The Indians are putting up a sail. They are trying to make off with Captain Oldham's boat!"

It was true. A canoe, heavily loaded with trade goods, set out toward Block Island, two miles away, but fourteen of the Indians remained on board the pinnace. They headed toward the mainland.

Captain Gallop raced aft, seized the tiller, and put his barque about. "Keep her north, northeast, Peter. We'll cross their bows on this tack. Sam, help me load our guns. We've only two fowling pieces and two pistols. Nothing but duck shot. Only the three of us to fight more than a dozen savages. Never mind. Those savages are not going to get away with that boat."

When the guns were loaded, Peter was sent forward with one

fowling piece. Captain Gallop took the tiller. "You're a good helmsman, Peter. But this takes better than good handling. Don't fire till I give the word. Then aim, lad—aim, and don't miss!"

On came Captain Gallop's barque, closer and closer. The Indians were clumsy inexperienced sailors, but if they had been experts, they could not have avoided that encounter. Peter saw that the savages stood ready with guns, pikes and swords. "Fire!" came the shout from Captain Gallop. Peter and Sam let fly among the savages, and every Indian turned and scuttled down the hatches, leaving the deck clear, though blood-stained.

Peter found himself shouting madly, "Have at them, have at them!" He seized the huge pistol, and emptied it at the last disappearing head.

Now the barque drew off, and there was a chance to re-load while she came about. This time Captain Gallop drew in so close that he "stemmed her upon her quarter," as he described it afterwards, and "almost overset her," which frightened the Indians so much that six of them jumped over-board.

The sail was flapping aboard the poor pinnace now, as she drifted helplessly, for all the savages were below hatches. Not one had the courage to come out and sail the ship.

Captain Gallop stood off again. "What we need is grappling irons, boys," he declared. "We can't manage to stay alongside long enough to rout those varmints out of there." His eye fell on the anchor. "I have it!" he cried. "Fasten our old mud hook to our bow; that'll turn the trick. It'll act as a ram, and like as not, it'll hold us to the enemy." Without more ado, he showed the boys how to fasten the anchor in place. They were both somewhat mystified, still, as to its purpose, but they were not

He struck her fair and square.

long in doubt.

Captain Gallop bore down on the pinnace, and this time he did not swerve to pass her close. He struck her fair and square. There was a splintering of wood, and the point of the anchor stuck fast. "Fire, boys, fire!" shouted the captain. "Rake her fore and aft! Get her between wind and water!"

It seemed futile to Peter to fire duck shot at the pinnace, for there was not an Indian on deck. He realized, however, that Captain Gallop wanted him to hit the boat below the deck, but above the water line. He did as he was told. To his surprise, the shots sank through the wood, and howls could be heard, showing that some of the savages inside the boat were hit.

"It's nought but inch plank," cried Sam. "Let 'em have it!" His face was black with powder. He was working like mad to load both guns, for he was better used to handling them than Peter. They fired several more rounds, but the anchor pulled loose and the boats began drifting apart again. Peter noticed that the wind was rising.

Now, as they stood off to come about, four more Indians jumped over-board. "That leaves but four savages on board, at the most," declared Captain Gallop. "We three are a match for them. Come on! Next time I'll try to drive our prow deeper, and we'll board."

The captain was as good as his word. This time the anchor-armored prow of the barque bit deep into the thin planks of the pinnace. "Boarders away," shouted Captain Gallop, brandishing one of the pistols. He leaped to the deck of Oldham's boat, Peter and Sam close at his heels.

Two of the Indians surrendered immediately, and Captain Gallop ordered Sam and Peter to tie them up. "Oldham!" he shouted down the hatchway. "Oldham, we're coming!" He descended the steep companion-way cautiously, his cocked pistol ready. He came back again almost at once, however, and Peter saw that his face was white and very grim. "They got him, lads," he said. "We're too late. Those bloody savages have murdered Captain Oldham, and they have robbed and mutilated his body. No use going below, boys—only make you sick."

"What—what about the two Indians below?" asked Peter, in a rather shaky voice.

"They've each got a sword, and they've barricaded themselves in a cabin," said Captain Gallop. "No use bothering with them—they can't get away. Find rope, boys. I'm going to tow this boat home to Boston—with all her freight in her, living and dead."

The boys silently fell to work. It had been a hot fight, while it lasted, but now a reaction set in. Peter felt cold, and sick at heart. "These must be the kind of Indians Red Fox was telling us about. They're not peaceful people, engaged in trading furs: they're thieving, murdering cut-throats. And my father is among them! And my friends, the Wests, are going to the Connecticut!"

They finally made the tow line fast, but Captain Gallop shouted at them to hurry more than once, for the skies were threatening. There was a good wind, and they set sail for Boston by noon, but the pinnace hung at their heels like a dead weight, holding them back.

Night came on, and with it, more wind. They were still only opposite the Narragansett shore. Now, it was plain that they were in for a storm. Captain Gallop hung on as long as he could, but at last he saw that their lives and both ships were in danger,

111

if he continued to tow the pinnace any farther. "Cut her loose," he shouted, above the roaring of the wind.

The pinnace disappeared almost immediately in a smother of wind and rain. One white glimmer of the ghostly sail, flapping in the dark—and she was gone. "What will become of her," Peter wondered. "She'll founder—with no one at the tiller—or she'll crash on the rocky shore, if she stays afloat so long. There'd be a sailor's grave for Captain Oldham."

But now the barque was by no means safe. She was driving ahead into the black dark, with not a star to show her the way home. "Listen for breakers, boys," cried Captain Gallop. "Aloft with you, Peter, and sing out if you see a line of white."

Somehow, the night wore through. With the first gray light of dawn, Captain Gallop knew where they were, though how, was a mystery to Peter. He tacked toward the shore. And then, with high seas still running outside, they began to find themselves in calmer, sheltered waters. They slid past some islands into the mouth of a little river, and the land locked them in. They cast anchor. "Now for some food and rest, boys," said Captain Gallop. "You look done in."

They ate what they had with them, and they slept, turn and turn about. "We set a watch," Captain Gallop explained. "We don't all go to sleep at once on board my barque, no matter how friendly we think the Indians may be."

Toward afternoon, Sam proposed that he and Peter should go ashore to hunt. Captain Gallop hesitated, but finally agreed, for in fact, the supplies were low. "If Peter may have one fowling piece, sir," said Sam, "I will trust to my bow and arrow. He is sure to get some ducks along the river bank, and I might possibly bring us something better."

The boys set out. Peter was rested, now. He felt his spirits rise at the prospect of hunting. To Sam, starting out for game was a commonplace chore, but Peter had never been hunting in his life. He tried to do just as Sam directed, but to his great annoyance, he had to be cautioned frequently against making noise. He simply could not seem to help it. A fallen branch that Sam crossed silently enough would snap and crackle under his feet, as though an army were passing.

They topped a knoll, and looked over. In the marsh below, ducks were peacefully swimming. Peter edged as much closer as he dared, then fired. To his immense satisfaction, the scattering duck shot took toll of several.

As Peter gathered up his game, Sam seemed to be searching for something in the mud along the banks of the little creek. At last he gave a grunt of satisfaction.

"What is it?" said Peter, who saw nothing interesting in the mud.

"Why, deer tracks, of course," Sam explained. "Don't you see them? Let's take cover, and wait. Perhaps a buck will come to water. No, no, not there" (as Peter started for some hemlocks). "Down the wind—over here."

The boys crossed the stream, and were about to conceal themselves on the other side, when Sam grasped Peter's arm and pointed. "Tracks, again—but not deer tracks—Indian tracks. H'm," said Sam, gazing intently, "not Narragansett, certainly."

"Why," gasped Peter "how can you tell?"

"Oh, by the shape of the moccasin, of course. Red Fox taught me. But I'm not a good tracker. I can't tell what tribe this is, for the life of me. Now why should a strange Indian be in Narragansett country. I don't like it. Let's get back to the boat."

13 : CAUGHT

PETER turned to go back down the river bank, but Sam stopped him. "Not that way!" he urged. "They can see us plainly. Let's cut across the ridge, where there's cover."

"They!" exclaimed Peter, glancing fearfully over his shoulder. "I thought you saw the tracks of just one savage!"

"I did, but that doesn't prove anything. Come on—we can't stay here."

Peter followed Sam toward the ridge, through rocky, broken country. After a few steps, it seemed to him as if the vast wilderness had swallowed them up. He tried to slip from tree to tree, the way Sam did, and gradually both boys' confidence returned. They saw no one, and they were taking good care not to be seen.

They came to a marsh, which had to be skirted cautiously before they could proceed. Peter felt hopelessly lost, but Sam was sure he knew which way to go. It began to grow dark.

"Right over the next ridge is the barque," declared Sam confidently.

But it was not. Sam paused to look again at the setting sun. "I have our direction right, haven't I, Peter?"

Peter had learned a great deal about piloting a ship at sea, and city streets were no mystery to him, but he found these woods utterly bewildering. "Your guess is better than mine, Sam," he replied. "You lead—I don't know where we are."

When they had mounted a third ridge, however, Peter stopped and sniffed. "I smell the sea." He pointed to the left.

Sam looked puzzled. "Should be the other way," he muttered. Then his face cleared. "I know. We're on a point of land. The best thing to do now is find the shore, and then follow it back to the barque. Maybe I should have done that in the first place, and taken a chance on being seen. We'd be back now, if I had."

Peter was too busy looking ahead through the trees for a glimpse of Long Island Sound to bother to reply. The boys plunged on, and suddenly—almost too suddenly—they came out on a cliff overlooking the water. "Phew!" gasped Peter, jumping back. "I'd hate to stumble on this place in the dark." Then he clutched Sam's arm, and pointed. There, out on a reef, left high and dry by the tide, was the wreck of a pinnace. "Captain Oldham's boat!" Sam nodded.

The boys stood looking out at the little ship and thinking of the last time they had seen her. It seemed a miracle that she was not at the bottom of the sound. She was dismasted, to be

115

sure. She was fast on the rocks, with doubtless a hole in her side —but it was the same brave little pinnace, in spite of everything.

"We'll tell Captain Gallop," said Sam. "Maybe he can save her." The same thought was in Peter's mind. The boys began to climb down the cliff without further hesitation.

"What about those Indians we left on board, Sam?" asked Peter, as they reached a little strip of sand that lay at the foot of the cliff. "Captain Gallop said there were two below decks, each with a stolen sword. Are they still there, do you think?"

"Of course not," said Sam, confidently. "The two we bound were drowned for certain. As for the other two—either they were drowned when the ship struck, or they got away long ago."

The boys turned southwest along the shore. They could see waves breaking on the rocks at the tip of the point. "Our barque is just on the other side, I'm sure," declared Sam.

Peter shouldered his ducks and the heavy fowling piece with renewed strength. How good the game would taste, roasted over a camp fire, alongside the barque! "We're almost there," he agreed. "I remember those islands."

They reached the end of the point, at last. A cliff rose steeply above them, and they were forced to wade among rocks, slippery with sea weed. An exclamation from Peter, and Sam turned in time to see his friend slip on a bunch of seaweed, clutch at a rock and finally fall with a splash into a foot or two of water. Peter rose, laughing, but when he saw that he had soaked Captain Gallop's fowling piece with salt water, he grew serious.

"Never mind," said Sam. "We were not going to use it again

tonight, anyway. I'll help you clean it after we reach the barque."

Peter picked up the gun, and drained the water out of it as best he could. As he did so, he noticed a deep cleft in the rocks under the cliff. It was formed partly by fallen rock from above, and partly by action of the sea. "Look, Sam!" he exclaimed. "A cave!"

Sam turned to look, and at that moment, an evil savage face peered out from the dark hole, then disappeared. For one dreadful instant the boys stood spellbound with terror. Then Sam whispered, "Come on! Look straight ahead. Pretend you saw nothing." The boys started to walk boldly past the cave, though both of them were inwardly terrified. As they got opposite, Peter could not resist stealing a glance out of the corner of his eye. He saw a menacing figure crouching among the rocks. It was an Indian with a sword in his hand. Behind him was another savage, and he, too, carried a white man's naked blade.

"If they rush us, threaten them with the gun," said Sam, speaking very low. "Maybe they don't know it's useless with the wet. If they keep on coming, I think I can stop them with my bow and arrows. Don't you pay any attention to me, though; you just run straight on around the point. I've got three good arrows —I ought to bring down one of those murderers—maybe both. But if I fail, I'll cut back and make for the woods."

"I'll stick with you," said Peter. "You're not giving yourself a chance, if you miss."

"Don't worry. I won't miss all three shots, and I can do better in the woods alone, without you."

"Are you sure they'll bother us?"

"Wait till we have our backs turned; then we'll know. They think we didn't see them, so we have a chance. Don't turn to look—don't run—yet."

Peter tried to walk as calmly and nonchalantly as Sam was doing, and he succeeded, although he did not realize it himself. Suddenly he heard something, or he felt something behind him, he could not tell which. "Look out! here they come!" Peter spun around, and raised the useless gun.

"Stop, or we'll shoot!" cried Sam, first in English—then in Narragansett. He pulled out one of his three precious arrows, and fitted it to his bow. One of the Indians hesitated, but then they both came on, leaping over the rocks toward the boys. They yelled, jeeringly.

"It's no use—they know too much about guns," thought Peter, but he kept on pointing the fowling piece. How he blamed himself for his accident in wetting the powder!

Sam took quick aim, and let fly at the nearest savage. Seemingly without effort, the Indian stepped aside, and the arrow flew harmlessly by him. Sam had the anguish of seeing the other Indian stoop and pick up that arrow, and add it to his own supply.

"Run, Wunx!" Sam cried. "See you at the boat!" Then he dashed straight at the oncoming savages, caught them by surprise, and managed to slip between them. They both turned to chase him, but Peter let out a wild, taunting yell of defiance. It was such a shout as he had often used for plaguing constables back in London, and it had its effect here, as well. Both Indians stopped to look at him. Sam took instant advantage and let fly his second arrow. This time, a howl of pain showed that he had found a mark.

Sam took quick aim and let fly at the nearest savage.

The Indian was only wounded, however. He set out after Sam, spoiling for revenge. The second savage decided that Peter was easier prey. He turned, and came bounding over the rocks.

For a time, Peter did very well, jumping from rock to rock, hiding behind ledges, twisting and turning, but always getting a little nearer the cove where the barque lay. The heavy fowling piece hampered him badly, and he finally had to abandon it, but he made sure he dropped it in deep water where the Indian would probably never find it. The ducks he had dropped long before, hoping the savage would delay to pick them up—which he did.

This was a different kind of running from any Peter was used to, however. There were no houses to dash through—in the front, out the back—no twisting lanes, no wharves to hide under. It was growing rapidly darker as the summer day drew to an end, and Peter missed his footing once or twice. The Indian seemed to be gaining on him, no matter how fast he went. The savage seemed utterly tireless. He leaped from rock to rock as easily as a wildcat, and his keen, black eyes seemed to see Peter instantly, wherever he hid to catch his breath.

Still, Peter might have escaped, but for a deep crevice in the rocks where the sea came in, splashing and breaking with a hollow sound. Peter was obliged to climb down, cross, and climb up again on the other side, while the Indian leaped easily across the top.

Now Peter knew how a rabbit must feel, with a hawk swooping down upon him, or with a dog upon his trail. He ran pluckily, however, wondering how soon an arrow would find his heart—but none came. Only light footsteps close behind—then arms with a grip like iron. He was thrown down hard on the rock.

120

He struggled—almost slipped, eel-like—from the Indian's grasp, but a hand at his throat squeezed and squeezed till everything went black, and Peter lay still.

Peter had only fainted, however. He came to a few minutes later to find himself bound hand and foot with leather thongs. Even then, he managed to remember what Sam had once told him: "Never show fear before an Indian." He stared up into the unwinking black eyes above him, and somehow he managed to hide the terror in his heart.

The Indian gave a grunt of satisfaction, hoisted the trussed-up Peter to his shoulder, as if he had been a freshly-killed deer, and set off through the forest with him. As the woods closed about them, Peter felt a wave of despair. It seemed to him that near the shore he had a chance, but the sea he loved was growing rapidly farther and farther away. "Oh, my father," he thought, tears stinging his eyelids. "How shall I ever find you now?"

14: THE INDIAN TOWN

AT first, Peter was too frightened and miserable to think. He shut his eyes to drive away the nightmare of events. Then the strong odor of rancid bear's grease, with which the Indian's back was coated, almost overpowered him. He opened his eyes again, but he was slung head downward, and he saw nothing but a dizzy, jolting confusion of tree roots. Gradually, as his brain cleared, it occurred to him that his captor was traveling very cautiously. "I believe he is in enemy country," thought Peter. "He's no Narragansett, I'm sure. If only one of Red Fox's people would come, I might be rescued."

Peter began to remember things Sam had told him. Beyond the Narragansett country, is a river—the Pequot River. All around the Connecticut are hostile Indians—Pequots. Now, he understood Red Fox's warning. "As sure as fate," he told himself, "Pequots murdered Captain Oldham, and a Pequot has captured me."

It grew very dark, and finally, the Indian stopped. He threw Peter, still bound hand and foot, under some thick hemlock branches. Then he pulled a piece of dried meat from a little sack, and began to eat. He did not offer Peter any food.

Peter did not care; he was suffering from thirst. "Water," he said. "I want water." How he wished he could speak Indian language, like Sam! The Pequot made no sign. It was too dark to see his face. "Water!" begged Peter again. This time a hard palm closed down over Peter's mouth. Peter said no more.

In spite of the leather thongs which bit into his flesh, and in spite of thirst, and insects which tormented him, Peter slept. There was a gray light in the sky when he was kicked awake once more. For a moment, he thought he was back at the inn; then he remembered. The Indian undid the knots around Peter's ankles, but he left his hands tied behind his back, and he made a slip noose which he put around the boy's neck.

"You walk now," he said in English, to Peter's surprise.

"Let me drink," Peter asked eagerly. He could hear the murmur of a brook near by, and the sound intensified his thirst.

The Pequot let him go forward along the trail to a place where a little stream crossed—let him kneel and put his face almost to the water. Then the Indian jerked on the noose around Peter's neck and pulled him back, nearly strangling him.

"Oh, so that's the game," thought Peter. His anger helped him to conceal his pain and disappointment. "Well, I won't let him have any more fun with me that way, if I die of thirst."

"Come on," he said with pretended carelessness. "You say walk—let's walk, then." He sensed that the Indian was rather

123

pleased with him, though his face did not change expression.

They traveled all day, and several times Peter's master offered to let him drink, only to jerk him back from the water just before his lips touched it. Peter, by a supreme effort of self-control, pretended not to care. At nightfall, he was at last allowed to drink his fill.

Very early next morning, they crossed a small glade, where bright green blades of corn were growing, and the marks of a hoe showed that someone had recently been at work. For an instant, Peter's heart leaped with hope. Was this a white man's settlement? But he saw no house—only, above the trees, wisps of smoke were rising as though from many camp fires. Now the path under their feet grew wider, and suddenly they came out on the high bank of a river. Directly across was a great fence built of tree trunks. It seemed to be in the form of a huge oval, with no gate in it at all. The Pequot led Peter down a steep, winding path to the water. He untied Peter's arms, but kept the thong tight about the boy's neck. Then he plunged into the river.

Peter allowed himself to be dragged through the water, choking and gasping. He could swim just as well as the Indian—but why let his captor know that! In midstream, he pretended to be in a panic of fright, hoping his struggles might make the Pequot let go the thong—but it was of no use. The sole result was that Peter swallowed more water than he wanted, this time, and the Indian, in an evil humor, kicked and jerked him up the bank.

A fierce barking of dogs broke out as they arrived at the top of the bluff. Now they were close to the big fence, and Peter could see that one end of it, instead of meeting to form a circle, overlapped the other, with a space of about two feet between. To enter, you turned sharply to the right, then a few feet farther

124

on, you turned left around the other end. This small space was piled high with dry brush, the purpose of which puzzled Peter greatly. He was to learn the meaning of it soon enough.

Peter's master let out a long, low call which was evidently a signal, for several women came running to pull the brush away from the entrance. Peter's master did not deign to notice these women, but he jerked Peter about to impress them.

Inside the palisade there was a cluster of small, dome-shaped huts, covered with bark. A few were larger, shaped like split cylinders, and evidently belonging to important warriors. The largest house of all stood in the center, and a group of Indians lounging about showed that it was a sort of public meeting place. Peter's master dragged him to one of the smallest bark huts, pulled up the deerskin that hung over the door, and threw him inside. The hut was dark and smoky, but Peter saw that a woman sat by a little fire, feeding a child from a wooden bowl. The child cried out at the suddenness of Peter's arrival, but the woman silenced him.

"Sannup!" exclaimed the woman.

The Pequot spoke a word or two to his squaw, then strode outside. Peter sat up. He could see his Indian master talking to the group of warriors outside the Long House. He was showing them his sword, and evidently telling of his adventures. Soon a crowd of braves gathered. A man came out of the Long House and everyone made way for him. "Their chief," thought Peter. "My Indian is making a great impression. I think the one who went after Sam has not arrived." Yet Peter scarcely dared to hope that Sam had gotten away.

The Squaw put her child on a bed made of skins stretched on a frame. It was very low—merely a foot from the ground.

She gave the baby a necklace of shells to play with, and then she set about plucking a wild pigeon. Several more of these birds lay on the dirt floor of the hut, and Peter picked one up and began to pluck it. Anything was better than sitting there idly, wondering what was going to happen to him, and worrying about Sam. "The cook at the King's Head taught me to do this," he thought to himself, as he quickly finished one bird, and reached for another. "I wonder what he would say, if he could see me now."

The squaw watched what Peter was doing, but whether she approved or not, he could not tell. She made no sign. Peter finished the birds. "I'm hungry," he said to her. "Can I have something to eat?"

The woman evidently did not understand, so Peter made signs. She took up a wooden bowl, filled it from a stone pot by the fire, and handed it to him.

Peter drank the hot broth, and it put new courage into him. It was well that it did, for his brief moment of peace and security was now over. His Indian captor, Sannup, and the other braves had completed their plans for torturing the young prisoner. It was an almost invariable Pequot custom. Narragansetts with terrible scars sometimes staggered back to their people, and told tales. More often, the tortured prisoner did not survive to tell, but his enemies boasted to frighten other tribes into submission. And when an unfortunate Pequot was, in turn, captured—the tales were remembered.

Peter did not know all this. In time, all the settlers knew it only too well, but that day had not yet come. He walked confidently into the space before the Long House. Hands seized him and threw him into the air—pretended to let him fall—then caught him. Peter clenched his teeth. "This is just to scare me," he thought. But the next time he was not caught. The Pequots let him fall on ground tramped hard with many a war dance, and Peter thought that all his bones were broken. They threw him till he began to hope his next fall would be his last.

Finally Peter received a blow which knocked him unconscious. He had a few moments of blessed oblivion. This did not suit the Pequots, however, and they were past masters at reviving a fainting victim. Peter came to with a scream of pain—the first protest he had uttered. They had brought him around by throwing hot coals on his chest.

He leaped up, but a hundred hands seized him and he was bound, hand and foot.

He closed his eyes, and some words of prayer his mother had taught him came into his mind. At this moment a young woman shoved her way into the crowd. Peter, sensing an interruption, opened his eyes, and saw that it was his captor's wife. "Sannup!" she cried to her husband, "stop them! I want that boy for a slave. Don't let them kill him."

Of course, Peter could not understand the woman's words, but he felt that she was on his side.

An old woman protested. "Be silent, Cohonk, lazy daughter of unlucky parents. Go to your lodge, and nurse your brat."

All the Indians laughed and applauded the old woman—all, that is, except Sannup. He had been just about to tell Cohonk to mind her own business, but now he took her side. "The prisoner is mine," he declared, "and if Cohonk wants a slave, she shall have one." To emphasize his words, he flourished his white man's sword—which all respected—and cut Peter's bonds. Peter, however, was by no means free. A crowd of angry Indians surrounded him, arguing violently.

15 : A CLOSE CALL

THE quarrel over Peter raged fiercely. Sannup had only a few on his side—mostly his wife's relatives—but he had his newly-acquired sword, which made a powerful argument. He brandished it in all directions, and managed to clear a space around his captive. Peter felt Cohonk's hand on his wrist. She was quietly maneuvering him nearer to her lodge. Now as the quarrel increased, the subject of it was practically forgotten, and finally Cohonk saw her chance. She slipped out of the press, Peter firmly in tow, and smuggled him into her hut before any-one noticed he was gone.

Once inside, she smeared Peter's burns with pine rosin, which, to his surprise, gave him relief. Then she let him sleep in a corner while she stood guard at the door, determined that not even the chief, Sassacus, himself, should take away her property. She resolved to build a new and bigger lodge on the morrow, for now she considered herself a person of importance. She smiled to think how the other women would envy her. As soon as Peter was able to crawl about, she set him to work.

Peter had been accustomed to hard work all his life. He was quick to learn, and he became so well worth his keep that Sannup took all the credit for having saved his life. His English clothes were taken from him and adapted in various ridiculous ways to Sannup's ceremonial costume. Cohonk dressed Peter Indian fashion. She talked to him as one would to a dog, teaching him simple words of command. Her little son was just learning to speak, however, and she talked to him carefully in simple language. Peter discovered that he could really learn Pequot by listening while Cohonk taught her child. Peter had a great deal of native shrewdness; he determined not to let anyone know how well he was beginning to understand the language.

He learned that "Cohonk" meant wild goose, and that "Sannup" signified fighter. The little child was called Gungumb, which meant big man! The little boy was proud of his name, and tried to live up to it.

At first Peter watched anxiously for Sam, fearing each day that he would be brought in and tortured. As time went by, however, and Sam did not appear, he decided that his friend must have been killed. He tried not to think too much about his father. Perhaps the Pequots had killed him, also. Or, he might be a prisoner in another Pequot town. Peter wanted to believe that his father was safe in Saybrook, but he found it hard to feel sure of anything any more.

As soon as Peter's bruises were gone, he began to think about

129

escape. It looked easy. There was no gate to the palisade—why not just walk out and away? He set out on the first dark night. When he reached the palisade entrance, he found this small space piled high with brush, as it had been the morning he was brought to the village. His foot struck a branch, and the crackling aroused every dog in the enclosure. They had been taught to guard that gate, and they were doing it.

Instantly Peter realized his danger. If he were caught at the gate, he knew Cohonk could never save him a second time. He darted back into the darkest shadows he could find. Some of the dogs ran up, yelping and snapping, but Peter drove them away and slipped inside the lodge. He almost collided with Sannup, who was rushing out to look for the enemy. All over the village, men snatched weapons, lighted pine torches and prepared for an attack. Peter lay down in his corner, his heart beating fast.

After this, Peter realized that escape was far from easy. The longer he lived among the Pequots, the more he came to respect their skill, their strength and their endurance. How could an English boy of thirteen expect to get away from this savage tribe unaided?

But Peter was not as utterly friendless as he supposed. One day a most unexpected sight met his eyes. He saw a small English vessel cautiously finding her way up the Pequot River. White men! Traders! He had almost forgotten that such things existed. He rushed to the bluff above the river, along with a crowd of excited Indians, and when he got a good look at the boat, he could not help shouting for joy. It was the *Bachelor* beyond a doubt.

She came nearer now, and Peter could see a broad-shouldered, strongly-built lad at the tiller. The breeze lifted his fair hair from his forehead. He turned his head in a way that Peter still remembered. Sam! Sam was alive, and well. He had come for Peter.

The boat swung close to the shore, and Peter began to push his way among the crowd of Pequots on the path leading down to the river. "Sam! Oh Sam!" he shouted, his voice sounding small and thin in the space that divided them. Then strong arms seized Peter from behind. A hand went over his mouth, stifling his cries, and he was carried away, kicking and struggling.

Peter was tightly bound, gagged and hidden under a deer-skin in the darkest corner of Sannup's hut. He owed his life to his having been useful to Cohonk, so that she wanted him for a slave, but this very fact worked against him now. Cohonk had seen the traders' vessel, and she had sent her husband to find Peter before the white men should discover him. She had no intention of losing her new slave. He was her proudest possession.

Sam came ashore to barter with the Indians. With him came a tall, gray-haired man, who seemed more interested in wandering about the Indian village than in trade. He looked into several bark houses, apparently from idle curiosity. When he approached Sannup's hut, however, the squaw set her dog on him. He went back to Sam and mentioned this.

Sam nodded. He had purchased a few furs, and now he began to make casual-sounding inquiries. Had anyone seen an English boy? He would pay a good price for a captive white boy—if they had one.

Sannup rose and went to his hut. The other Pequots received

Sam's questions in stolid silence. Then Sannup returned, scowling. "How much for pale-face boy? Me no got—but how much?"

Sam offered an axe and two knives. Sannup shook his head. Sam added a length of blue cloth, and Sannup went back to his lodge. When he returned, he was still scowling. "Me no got," he repeated.

"Down the river they told us a mighty warrior had a pale-face slave here," Sam persisted, hoping to appeal to Sannup's vanity. "Suppose I offer you all these things, and—" he drew forth his mother's copper kettle—"and even this!" Sam could hear a faint rustle among the watching Indians. This was a splendid offer. Sannup scowled, and went to his lodge once more.

As for Peter, when Sannup came into the lodge, he was able to understand most of what passed. He heard Sannup say that two white traders had come. One was Sam, Peter knew—but the other? Not Captain Webber; he would never leave the *Bachelor* unguarded. Who, then? A wild hope sprang up in his heart. "Can it be my father?" he thought. He tried to struggle, to cry out—but he could not. He heard Cohonk refuse the offer to sell her slave.

Sannup went out. Peter heard voices in the distance. Then the Indian came back again. Peter heard him say the white men were offering a copper kettle now. Cohonk hesitated. Peter knew this must be the kettle that Sally had given to Sam, bidding him get plenty of furs for it. Peter might be a captive and a slave, but he was not without friends. He listened with beating heart, while Sannup urged his wife to trade.

"Why trade," said Cohonk. "Why not kill the traders and

take their goods. You killed before—kill again."

Sannup went out, but Peter had ceased to think about his own freedom. If only he could contrive to warn his friends! He struggled fiercely. The thongs cut deeply into his wrists.

Sannup returned. "The chief says we will not kill. These men are watchful, not like the others. Will you sell your slave?"

"No," said Cohonk. Peter had endured torture, hard work and frequent beatings without a murmur, but now, in the darkness under the deerskin, the tears rolled down his face.

Cohonk untied Peter's bonds as soon as the *Bachelor* was well out of sight. He sat staring into the fire, gnawing a bone she had given him for supper, and thinking hard. It must be tonight, he decided, before the *Bachelor* had gone too far down river. He crept off to his corner and waited a long time, pretending to sleep.

At last, he rose. He did not stop to steal food. Instead, he took down two long, coiled deerskin thongs that hung on the center pole of the hut. It was bright moonlight outside, and Peter crouched in the black shadow of the lodge for a while, listening. No one stirred. Then he crept cautiously toward the palisade, on the side nearest the river. He avoided the brush-filled entrance, for he had learned his lesson. When he reached the spot he had chosen, he paused, and looked up at the top of the great twelve-foot fence. It was built of trees sunk deep in the ground, and set close together. All the branches had been lopped off, and the sides of the wall were as smooth as glass.

Peter did not hesitate, however. He uncoiled the two long thongs he had brought from Sannup's lodge, and quickly knotted them together. Then he fastened a stone to one end of the thong, and tried to throw it over the top of the palisade.

133

Each of the great logs in the barrier had been cut to form a point at the top. This was to make the wall more difficult to climb over, but Peter meant to lodge his stone in the cleft between two logs. The first time he cast the thong, the stone at the end fell short. He tried again. This time it came down just over the top, between two pointed logs. He pulled it carefully, to make the stone lodge tightly. "Now," he thought, "if only the thong is strong enough to bear my weight!"

The moonlight shone full upon him, for the sky was cloudless. There was nothing to do but go ahead. He took a tight grip on the thong, and started to pull himself up the fence, just as he had so often climbed the mast on board the *Bachelor*.

There came a low laugh, and Peter felt his legs seized in a vice-like grip. The thong broke, and Peter fell to the ground. Instantly someone rolled him over, and tied his hands with the broken thong. He sprang up, but a blow from a heavy stick brought him down. "That will teach you, little snake," he heard Cohonk whisper. "Be silent and come with me, or I will give the alarm. Then the braves will come and kill you, little fool. I will beat you myself, but I will not kill you—not this time. After this, you shall work so hard you will fall asleep in your tracks. You shall not make plans at my fireside again. I know—I saw you. Your white friends came for you, but you are mine, and I will not sell you, and you will not get away."

When Peter at last lay down in the hut again, his body was covered with bruises, but his will to escape was stronger than ever. "I shall think of a better way," he told himself. "Next time I shall succeed. I am Peter Cutler; I will not be an Indian's slave all my life!"

Meanwhile, the *Bachelor* was anchored downstream. Sam

Peter felt his leg seized in a vice-like grip.

was talking to the tall man who had come ashore with him. "I wish you would let me try, Mr. Cutler," he was saying. "I feel sure Peter is there, and I want to try to steal him away."

But Peter's father shook his head. "You would only lose your life, Sam. We must move slowly. First, we should put them off their guard, then think of a better plan."

He sighed. "If only I had seen the boy. I would give anything to know for certain he is alive. But I do not despair. Think of my own wonderful escape in the wilderness! When I lost the trail in the storm, and the falling tree pinned me to the ground, I might have lain there till I died. Instead, an Indian woman who was gathering roots heard my moans. She might have been a Pequot, and I might have been killed. But no. By God's Providence, I was found and cared for by Narragansetts. Your good friend Red Fox guided me back to your home, when my leg had healed. Surely, I could not come safe at last through so many perils, only to lose my Peter. We shall find him, never fear."

"He is there in that town," said Sam. "I am certain of it. But I will try to be patient—though I hate sailing away like this."

16 : MEN-AT-ARMS

PETER realized that he must allay suspicion before trying to escape again. This would take patience. From time to time he thought he saw an opportunity to run away, but he forced himself to wait and plan. Summer was drawing to a close, and the harvest was plentiful. Peter managed to hide a few kernels of corn every night. "I must have food," he said to himself. "There's no telling how far I may have to travel." He thought about the best route to take. Straight east through the forest? That way was shorter, but more dangerous. To the sea, and along the coast then? Perhaps.

As often as possible, Peter slipped over to the council fire to listen to the talk of the Indian braves. No one supposed he understood, but gradually, their language became more and more clear to him. "I must learn all I can about these people, if I am to outwit them and escape," he thought.

Sassacus, chief of all the Pequots, had been absent on a mission. When he returned, a council was called, and Peter crept to the outer edge of the circle of braves to learn what was afoot. With the chief was an Indian from Block Island; and just as Peter found a place in the shadows beyond the ring of firelight, this Indian leaped to his feet.

"It's all your fault," he cried, pointing at Sannup, Peter's master. "You killed the white trader, Oldham. Just because some of my tribe were fools enough to go with you, the English came and burned our village. They asked us for wampum, and more wampum. They spoiled our canoes. They burned our corn. And all because of you!"

"You are a woman," Sannup replied, insultingly. "You are afraid of the white men. Why did you hide when they came? Why did you shoot an arrow or two, and then run? Kill the white men, I say. Kill them all, and take their women and children for slaves!"

There was a murmur of approval all around the campfire. Peter felt his heart grow cold as he heard it. "The English wear magic coats," the Block Island Indian replied sullenly. "We shot our best arrows, but they fell to earth with broken points. I tell you, those coats are strong medicine. They shine in the sun, and they are better than flint for hardness."

Sannup grunted contemptuously, but some of the other warriors were impressed.

Sassacus arose. He was wearing a ceremonial blanket, and a headdress of eagles' feathers, which greatly increased his stature. His face was painted with bars of red and black, arranged to give him an expression of ruthless cruelty. He folded his arms and stood motionless in the firelight. The tribe fell silent.

When every eye was upon him, Sassacus began to speak. "Our brother Sannup is right. Kill the English! They have come to take this land, which we have won with our hearts' blood. Shall the spirits of our fathers stand by and see us yield like women? No! They bid us fight."

A fierce murmur of approval ran through the crowd. Sassacus continued: "When my wise men make magic, they see us driven forth, as of old. They bid us fight.

"So let us kill the English, as we would kill our enemies, the wolves—and take their pelts. I, Sassacus, your chief, will lead you. We will kill!" He raised his tomahawk in air, in one fierce gesture. "We will kill," he repeated, "till our river runs red with blood!"

Once more that fierce murmur of "Kill, kill," was heard among all the tribe, and Peter felt the clutch of fear at his throat. He stirred uneasily in the shadows, but he was careful to make no sound. He longed to get away to the comparative safety of Cohonk's wigwam, yet he must try to hear more.

"But our Island brothers are right, also," Sassacus continued. This time his words were received in cold silence. "It is true that the English warriors wear coats of powerful magic. We must wait until we have guns like theirs to turn against them.

"Here is my plan: At the mouth of the Connecticut is a white man's village. You have seen it. There are but few men there; hardly more English than the fingers of my two hands." He spread out his powerful hands in the firelight, then snapped his fingers contemptuously. "These men are weak. They are hungry. But they have guns, plenty of them. You have seen it?"

The circle growled assent. "Good," said Sassacus. "Now the Boston warriors have left the island and are at Saybrook. My scouts have told me. They wait for a wind to blow their boats, which are too big to paddle. Soon they will go home to their town without walls." He paused significantly, and Peter shuddered, as he realized how open to attack Boston really was.

But Sassacus went on. "When the ships have gone, we will burn Saybrook," he declared fiercely. "We will burn all the settlements on the Connecticut. We will arm ourselves with guns from the fort, and many slaves shall hoe our corn.

"Those squaw men, the Narragansetts, will join us. I, myself, shall deal with Miantonomoh, their chief. Let the Narragansetts burn Boston, Salem, Plymouth—all their towns."

A frenzy of excitement greeted this plan. Braves arose, shook their tomahawks in the air, then pounded them upon the ground, crying "Kill—kill the whites!" Sassacus folded his arms and watched them, but at exactly the psychological moment he spoke again.

"My brave brothers, wait. Have patience," he commanded. "Let these English who have come against the island go in peace. Believe me, that is best, for we must have guns, and the magic powder that makes them speak. Remember the guns we took from the stupid traders, so many moons ago? Now, they speak not. They are useless without this strange gray dust, and the little balls that look so weak, but are so mighty."

"So that's it," thought Peter. "They stole guns, but they can't shoot them. Well, that's one piece of good luck, at least."

"So wait, my brothers," continued Sassacus. "With the wisdom of the deadly rattlesnake, let us wait. Then strike to kill!"

Once more the warriors murmured among each other like angry bees. "He is right," they said. "Sassacus is a great chief; let us do as he says."

Peter crept into Sannup's lodge and lay down, but not to sleep. His heart was beating wildly, yet he forced himself to think. "There is no time to lose," he said to himself. "I must escape at once, and this time, I cannot fail. I must warn Lieutenant Gardiner, and save Saybrook!"

The next day, Peter was sent to the cornfield. He picked great baskets full of ripe ears of corn, and brought them to the village. All the women and children worked at gathering corn that day. They chattered gaily to each other, for the season had been a good one, and they were happy at the prospect of so much food. Suddenly a runner from the nearest village came padding up the trail into their midst. "The English men!" he cried out to them. "They come in many boats!"

The messenger ran on, leaving the utmost confusion behind him. At first everyone crowded to the river bank, but because of its winding course, no ships were to be seen. Then Peter found himself being hustled inside the village stockade, and he saw warriors run to the two entrances, carrying weapons. They did not stay there, however; they seemed to have no idea what to do.

Now a long shout went up from those still watching at the river. Peter, taking advantage of the confusion, ran outside the palisade. He saw three pinnaces sailing slowly around the bend. Behind them came a small Dutch trading vessel and a shallop. "Can all those men be coming to trade at this village?" thought Peter. Then he caught the glint of steel helmets and breastplates. Men at arms! "This is not trade—it's war!" he said to himself. He wanted to seize a musket and fight beside his own people; but he knew what he must do—hide quickly.

Peter turned and ran along the top of the bluff toward the cornfield, but it was already too late. Cohonk had seen him. Peter had a good start, but she could run like a deer. He had just time to hide in a thicket before she reached the cornfield. He saw her stoop and examine the hoed earth, pick out her slave's tracks among the many, and head straight for his hiding place. He lay still, but a blue jay above his head kept scolding and screeching. Cohonk laughed, and an instant later she was dragging him back to the village. "Now, I shall be bound and gagged as before," thought Peter. "Maybe my own people will shoot me, without my being able to tell them who I am."

He was not bound, however. Instead, Cohonk began to load all her worldly goods upon his back. She worked with feverish haste, tearing mats off the walls of the hut, gathering up wooden bowls and spoons, wrapping them in deerskin, and heaping all on Peter. Bundles began to slip, but she bound them tight with thongs.

The confusion had lessened somewhat in the village, and Peter saw the reason. Sassacus had come forth from the Long House, and was striding up and down, giving orders. "You are children," Sassacus shouted angrily. "Will you wait till the English are upon us? Go, each man to his task. Do as I say!"

The English vessels drew nearer and nearer. Cohonk worked with desperate speed, but at last, even she realized that Peter could carry no more. She picked up her soapstone cooking pot, sighed, and put it down. She began to dig frantically in the dirt floor of the hut. Then she buried the pot, and even some ears of corn snatched from the pile outside the door. But now the other women and children began silently leaving the village, and she dared delay no longer. She carried her little son in her arms, and ordered Peter to follow.

"Shall I put a thong around your slave's neck for you?" asked Sannup. He had been listening to the plans of Sassacus, but he joined his family when he saw they were ready.

Cohonk hesitated, then shook her head. "He can't run away with all that fastened on his back," she said.

They wound along a narrow trail eastward, away from the river. Sannup followed, some distance behind. His bow was in his hands, and his best arrow was notched on the string.

Before long they struck off the trail. The going was difficult. Suddenly Cohonk halted. Peter saw that they had reached a tiny glade surrounded by hemlocks. All around them were great gray rocks. If other women of the tribe were hidden near, they could not be seen. Sannup stayed long enough to make sure that his wife and child were safely hidden, like a doe with her faun; then he left them, and returned to his chief.

While Sannup and many of the others had been seeing to the safety of their families, Sassacus chose young warriors to meet the English. "Hide your weapons and go as if in peace," he instructed them. "Keep the dogs of English talking as long as you can." A young Pequot called Concomithus was put in charge, because he had spent a winter in Plymouth, and spoke English.

Concomithus took a canoe and went out to the pinnaces, which were now anchored in midstream, opposite the town. "Who are you, and what do you want?" he called in Pequot, for he rightly judged that he could prolong the parley by pre-

143

All around them were great gray rocks.

tending to speak nothing but his own tongue. To his disappointment, however, a Narragansett interpreter was called.

"So it's Cutshamakin," exclaimed the Pequot in pretended surprise. "I heard you were last seen hoeing corn, while your squaw took the war path."

Cutshamakin's eyes flashed, but when the English asked him to translate he pretended not to hear. "This is the great General Endicott, from Boston," said Cutshamakin, throwing out his chest. "He commands your chief, Sassacus, to stand forth."

"Sassacus, the mighty chief, has gone hunting," Concomithus replied, adding, "Do you call that little crowing cock of a white man a chief?" Again Cutshamakin omitted to translate.

"What does he say?" demanded Endicott. "Sassacus not here? They told us down the river that he was. Well, have them send for him."

Concomithus gravely promised to send for his chief. "Sassacus has gone to the place you English call Long Island," he lied glibly. "It will take a long time, but behold, I send a messenger." One of the young warriors in a canoe just behind Concomithus started paddling down the river, as if to find Sassacus. Another went to the shore to tell Sassacus what had been done.

The chief stood among a chosen band of his bravest warriors, looking down upon the English ships. "It is good," he said, when the messenger had reported. "Feed them with lies." He looked at the sun, and saw that it was already well past midday. A plan was in his mind, and it was a good plan, if only the English could be fooled into waiting. He had them deep in Pequot country, now. Would they possibly be such fools as to land their men, and then wait on shore till after dark? Sassacus did not know.

17 :   RETREAT

AS soon as the Pequot messenger set out down the river to make a pretense of finding Sassacus, General Endicott began to disembark his men. There were four captains with eighty volunteers from the Bay Colony and twelve men from Saybrook. Some were better armed than others, but to the savages, they presented an imposing array.

Sassacus watched them climb the steep bluff to the village. While his face showed only impassive calm, his heart was seething with rage. If only he had enough warriors ready to attack! If only his useless guns could be made to speak! The Englishmen were at such a disadvantage on that narrow path that he could almost have destroyed them all.

It was about three in the afternoon by the time Endicott had his force drawn up in the middle of the Pequot village. The rattle of drums ceased, and the captains gave the order to stand at ease. The soldiers began to glance curiously about them. Some had traded with Indians, and were familiar with the scene. Others had just come from the Old World, and everything looked strange to them. No Indian women or children stirred among the lodges, and some of the soldiers wondered why. The silence was uncanny. Not even a dog barked. More than one man-at-arms felt a sense of impending danger.

"Ask them how long before Sassacus comes," Endicott said to his interpreter.

Cutshamakin put the question, and the Pequots went to consult with Sassacus. He looked at the sky. "Tell them I come when the sun touches the tips of yonder pines." (This would take about three hours.) "Do not tell them quickly. Make a long pow-wow. When that much time has gone, tell them the same thing again."

Little by little, more Indians came silently from the forest. Where first there had been but a handful, now they gathered in alarming numbers. General Endicott estimated that there were about three hundred. For the first time he doubted the wisdom of landing his force in the Pequot town. In Boston, however, men talked contemptuously of savage strength in warfare. Endicott's experience at Block Island bore out this opinion. "Just a show of firmness," he thought. "That's all they require."

Some of the Indians went over to the rank and file of soldiers and started to talk with them. Now, as the shadows grew longer, Endicott began to have a feeling of uneasiness. He went to the lines where the Pequots were talking, and ordered them to keep their distance. They were unarmed, he noticed, and they obeyed him with seeming willingness. Yet something in their glance gave Endicott a sudden thrill of fear.

"You're Gardiner's men, aren't you?" he said to the soldiers. "Is that why these savages know you?"

"Yes, sir," said Thomas Hurlburt, speaking for the twelve men Lieutenant Gardiner had sent with the expedition. "We have traded with some of these Pequots at Saybrook."

"Well, what were they saying to you?" Endicott demanded irritably. "Did you get any idea when Sassacus will come back?"

"These Pequots are tricky, sir," said Hurlburt. "I never believe a word they say, myself. I think Sassacus is right here now, up to some kind of mischief. Now, Lieutenant Gardiner always says, 'Never stay ashore after dark among Pequots'— so if you don't mind my telling you, sir—"

Endicott snorted. "That'll do, that'll do."

General Endicott and his army of ninety-six men had just come from Saybrook Fort. They had been wind-bound there for several days, and during that time Endicott had plenty of opportunity to tell what he had done and what he meant to accomplish. "I have been especially commissioned by the Governor of the Bay Colony," he had said pompously, "to punish the murderers of Captain Oldham. The Indians of Block Island are now completely subdued, and I shall attend to those on the Pequot River as soon as this wretched wind changes."

"So you burned all the corn on the island," Lieutenant Gardiner had remarked. "And now, you come here and quarter your army on us, when we have not enough supplies. We are pleased to receive you, but you could have brought some of that corn with you. You could have carried some to Boston, where,

149

judging from the price, corn is scarce."

Endicott was very conscious of his own rank of general, and of the importance of his mission. "I am here to punish miscreants," he declared, "not to gather corn!"

"The miscreants must be punished," agreed Lion Gardiner. "But as I see it, when you sail back to Boston, the Pequots will be about our ears like hornets, and we shall be punished, most of all. If you must make war upon the Pequots, then give me leave to send men to gather corn. Food, munitions and men, remember. Not one of these three is more important than another."

Perhaps, in his heart, John Endicott knew the expedition was unwise. But Lion Gardiner was a mere lieutenant, although he was more experienced in war. Endicott's pride would not let him listen to advice, and now, when Thomas Hurlburt tried to advise him, he was annoyed all over again. "If I retreat to my boats," he thought, "these savages will think I am afraid." He turned on his heel and strode away.

At last it was nine o'clock. For the second time, Sassacus failed to appear at the hour appointed, and now everyone, including Endicott, felt a sense of danger, like a living thing coiled in the darkness. From somewhere outside the palisade came a low hoot, like an owl. Instantly every Indian faded out of sight into the shadows, except for four young braves—Sannup among them—who kept up a pretense of parley.

"Enough of this!" cried Endicott. "Cutshamakin, tell them I will not wait for Sassacus. I now make my formal demand of these four men here. Bring forth the murderers of Stone and his men. You are harboring Oldham's murderer as well. Deliver him, also, to English justice. We require one thousand fathoms of wampum in place of the paltry gift we returned to you previously. We demand the children of a chief as hostages against further outrages."

The four young warriors did not reply. Instead, they turned, and would have disappeared into the darkness like the rest, but Endicott shouted, "Halt!" When they did not halt, the English soldiers fired. Two of the Pequots fell, while two got away, wounded. Then a long, blood-chilling war whoop broke out all around the little army. It seemed to come from everywhere. The soldiers fired blindly at the shadows.

A shower of arrows rattled on coats of mail and steel helmets, but they fell harmlessly to earth. Only one soldier cried out in agony; he had been hit in the eye.

The English re-loaded and fired another round, but at an invisible foe. Then someone snatched a brand from the council fire, and ran with it to the Long House. In a few seconds, it was blazing fiercely, for it was made of dry bark. Others snatched brands, and ran shouting from lodge to lodge. The scene was as bright as day from the burning wigwams, but no women and children ran screaming forth. Endicott realized that they had all been safely hidden away. There was no use looting huts, either, as they had done on Block Island, for nothing of value remained.

The men now tried to burn the stacks of corn which had just been picked. It was too green, however, so they began to trample it into the ground, to spoil it.

Thomas Hurlburt rushed up to them. "Wait!" he cried. "You promised to help us load that corn in our bags and take it to the shallop. Stupid! Dolts! What are you doing? We are starving at Saybrook, and you are spoiling good food. Stop it,

I say. Why do you think Lieutenant Gardiner sent us with you, anyway!"

Hurlburt managed to make the soldiers leave the corn alone. He set four of his own twelve men to shoving the ears into bags. Lieutenant Gardiner had provided thirty new bags for the Boston men to fill for their own use. All he asked was that his men be aided in filling six bags for Saybrook. But the Boston men continued to burn lodges. "What do you take me for—a farmer?" shouted a man-at-arms. "I am a soldier—I don't gather grain."

Hurlburt's men, however, showed better discipline. They filled bags as fast as they could. Hurlburt allowed only four out of his command to do this. "Can't I help them, sir?" asked young William Chace, who had been ordered to stand guard.

Hurlburt shook his head. "Lieutenant's orders," he said. "Here, take Green's gun, as well as your own, and guard the path to the river."

By now the flames of the burning huts began to die down. Endicott realized that his men would soon be left in darkness again, and not even he imagined that the Pequots had really run away. He ordered the drummers to beat for retreat.

The rolling of drums reached the ears of Sassacus, as he crouched in the forest nearby. He saw that the white men were turning to march away. He signaled his followers. He would rally them once more, and assault the rear of the army. They prepared to attack with tomahawks, hand-to-hand.

When Thomas Hurlburt heard the signal for retreat, he was dumfounded. Endicott had promised Lieutenant Gardiner that he would protect the men who gathered corn. He had promised to see them all safely on board the shallop, first. Then, and not before, he had promised to withdraw his soldiers. Yet there they went—without warning.

Hurlburt, however, had remembered Lieutenant Gardiner's directions. He had divided his twelve men in three parts, exactly as ordered. Four men stood by the stacks of corn, their muskets ready. Four others guarded the path to the river, while the remaining four, who had handed their muskets to these guards, loaded sacks.

"Take what you've got and get out," shouted Hurlburt to those who gathered corn. "Run for our shallop. Stand ready, men!" he shouted to his guards. Then he glanced at the forest, just as Sassacus and his braves broke cover. "Here they come," he cried. "Fire!"

The muskets spoke, but when the smoke cleared away, only two Pequots lay on the ground. "Steady, boys," said Hurlburt. "We'll have to shoot better than that, if we get clear. Quick, men! Those with one rifle, run for the edge of the bluff; then re-load there. Try to find cover."

Hurlburt stopped at the palisade gateway. "One man can hold this," he said. "Chace and Bartlett, you go outside the gateway and cover my retreat, but don't shoot your last shot without a mark."

The Indians had fallen back, but how they came on again across the ruined village. Hurlburt waited until the foremost Pequot showed plain against the dying firelight; then he fired, and the leader dropped. Once more, the Indians fell back.

"Now," cried Hurlburt, re-joining Chace and Bartlett, "to the top of the bluff, all of you!" They ran, found shelter, and began to re-load. "Chace, Bartlett and I will stay here," Hurlburt ordered. "The rest of you, fire, then run for the boats. Can

153

you see where the men with the bags of corn are?"

"I see two, half way to the shallop, sir," said Bartlett.

"Good," said Hurlburt. "It's hard going in the dark." He heard a groan from the path just below. "What's that?" he cried sharply.

"It's me, sir—Green. One of them arrows got me in the thigh. I can make it, sir, only slow."

"Good man. Just keep going the best you can—we'll hold 'em. Look out! Here they come again!"

Four flashes showed where Hurlburt's men fired. "That stopped 'em," shouted Hurlburt. "Now run for the boats, you four!" To the two men left by his side, he said quietly, "Try to count ten, boys, before you fire."

Once more the Pequots had been checked; only two broke through the rim of bushes at the top of the bluff. They fired, but Hurlburt heard a low moan from one of the men at his side. He had no time to learn what it meant, for a savage loomed above him in the dark, and a great stone tomahawk came down on his shoulder. Hurlburt's steel shoulder guard gave out an angry clank. He clubbed his musket, and struck upwards; it was difficult, for the Pequot was above him, and had all the advantage. They fell together and rolled down the path among scattering stones. Somehow Hurlburt managed to hang on to his musket.

There was a flash close to his face. "Got him, sir," he heard Chace's voice. "Are you all right?"

"Yes," gasped Hurlburt. "Run for the boat. Where are the others?"

"All aboard, sir. Bartlett's hurt, but not badly. Come along, sir." Together they ran panting into the water, and clambered

One man fired and a shadowy figure dropped.

aboard the shallop. One of the men on board the boat fired, and a shadowy figure just behind them on shore dropped, and was still.

The three pinnaces, bearing Endicott and his men-at-arms, had already disappeared around the bend in the river. As Lieutenant Gardiner had prophesied, they had "raised a hornet's nest," and now they made off, leaving the Saybrook men alone.

"Pull on the oars, boys," Hurlburt shouted. "Make for the middle of the stream; we aren't out of danger yet, by any means!"

18 : NOW OR NEVER

OUT in the forest under the dark hemlocks, the rattle of muskets came faintly to the keen ears of Cohonk. She knew what it meant, and she turned to Peter, her black eyes blazing with anger. "If your people have killed my warrior," she hissed, "I will kill you—slowly. You will be dying little by little, for days and days."

The smell of smoke drifted down the wood. "They burn," Cohonk whispered. "Remember, oh my son. The English burn our home. When you are a man, remember. When your turn comes—kill and burn!"

The night passed slowly. Peter was intensely miserable, for Cohonk would not unbind his burden, lest they should need to flee farther, and also lest Peter should run away. He slept a little from sheer exhaustion, face down, upon the ground.

On the morning of the second day, Cohonk prepared a little food for herself and her child, but she gave none to Peter. She sat staring into space, brooding and silent, except when she roused herself to speak of vegeance. "Even if Sannup is alive," thought Peter, "the tribe will probably kill me for revenge."

By noon they heard the faint rustle of someone stirring. A warrior had come to take his family back to the ruined village. But the warrior was not Sannup.

The afternoon wore on. They heard other sounds, as one by one the families went home. The chill of evening crept through the woods, and still they waited. At last Cohonk made ready to leave alone. She spoke no word, but to Peter her silence was more terrifying than any further threats would have been. He knew she had given up hope. She felt certain that her warrior lay dead. So she was planning Peter's torture, step by step.

Silently, they filed into the ruins of the Indian village. Circles of ashes told where the huts had been. There was a sound of women wailing, and Peter saw a young girl snatch up charcoal and blacken her face with it. Then he saw four bodies stretched out where once the Long House had stood. Cohonk left him, and went to look.

Peter watched her, and at the same time, he struggled madly to get free of the thongs that bound the load upon his back. He could not loosen them. He saw Cohonk look once at the fallen braves, and then turn away. She did not wail. She did not blacken her face.

So Peter knew that Sannup had not been among the dead. The relief was so great that for a moment his knees felt weak as water, and he almost fell. But where was Sannup, then? He saw Cohonk go about asking her friends, searching for him.

At last another woman seemed able to help Cohonk. She pointed to the forest, talking rapidly. Cohonk disappeared, and soon Peter saw her emerge again, half leading, half carrying her warrior. He was badly wounded, and Cohonk helped him to lie near the spot where their lodge had been. Then she hastily undid the thongs on Peter's back. She selected a fine deerskin to lay over her husband. "Little fool, find the mats," she called to Peter. "Hurry up! Build a fire. Dig up my cooking pot and set it going."

Peter obeyed, while Cohonk leaned over her husband, examining his wound. In the village the medicine men were beginning to shake their rattles. An old woman came stumbling over to Cohonk's side. "Balsam to stop bleeding," she said, "witch hazel for bruises." She began laying on leaves.

Cohonk straightened, and looked at Peter. There was still such venomous hatred in that glance that he suddenly realized he was not safe, after all. If Sannup should die, her threats would be carried out—with interest. She laid her hand upon a thong, as if to bind Peter then and there. But she hesitated. "Take a bucket to the river and fill it, lazy one," she said, instead.

"That was a near thing," thought Peter. "When I get back with the water, she means to tie me up." He picked up the birchbark bucket.

The noise in the village increased as more members of the medicine lodge appeared. They danced in single file, in and out among the burned wigwams, shaking great rattles made of tortoise shells and beating snake-skin drums. "Oh Life God, save this dying warrior," they chanted, as they reached Sannup.

"Mother," said the little boy, pulling at Cohonk's deerskin

There was such a venomous hatred in that glance that

Peter realized he was not safe.

skirt. "Mother!"

"Hush," she whispered in his ear. "Do not disturb the medicine men."

"Your slave, Mother! He has fallen in the river, and he cannot swim!"

Cohonk started up with a cry of anger. Then she looked back at her husband. The medicine dancers had wound their way to another lodge, but the old woman remained. She was trying to close Sannup's wound with balsam resin. "Go for your slave, daughter," she said. "I can attend to this."

Cohonk rushed down the steep path to the river. In the gathering darkness, she saw Peter's dark head above the water for a moment. She marveled that he should be so far from shore. Then she saw his hands thrashing wildly, before he went down again. She ran to a canoe and pushed it into the water, but she uttered a cry of dismay as the dugout sank immediately. She tried another, but this, too, was useless. She realized that the English soldiers must have smashed the bottoms out of all the log canoes, just as they had done before, on Block Island. For a moment she thought of jumping into the river and swimming after Peter, but already she had lost many precious moments. It was too late—the boy was out of sight.

"Strange," she mused, angrily. "Why should he suddenly be so clumsy? I thought the brat could swim, too." Then her eyes narrowed with suspicion. "I will persuade one of our best trackers to search both shores for footprints tomorrow, as soon as the sun is up," she vowed.

19: NIGHT AND THE RIVER

PETER put on such a good imitation of a drowning boy that he swallowed considerable water, and nearly tired himself out. Fortunately, the Pequot River was a winding stream, and before long, the bluff on which the village stood was hidden from sight. Peter was able to float with the current, and rest.

The current carried him along rather swiftly. There were islands in the river, and Peter had to watch in the gathering darkness, lest he strike his head against a rock. He thought regretfully of the plans he had made to carry a little store of food in a bag, hung around his neck. There had been no time to take anything away. He wished that he could climb out of the water and run along the shore, just as a rest from so much swimming —but he knew better than to try it. There were Indian villages along the banks. If dogs should bark, he would be discovered, and caught. Perhaps he would be tortured at once in revenge for what the English had just done, or perhaps he would be returned to Cohonk. And that, Peter knew, would probably be the worst of the two evils.

The stars came out, one by one. Peter swam, rested, and swam again, for hours. He found himself thinking of Sam. "Sam did his best to get me away from them," he said to himself. "I suppose he gave up, and finally forgot about me, after that. I don't blame him. Well, Sam, here I come—or I hope I do!"

Peter began to feel desperately cold. He swam without stopping to rest to keep the blood coursing through his legs, although they felt as though they belonged to someone else. He had never stayed afloat in the water so long before in his life. His experiences in the wilderness, though harsh enough, had strengthened him, however. He had planned to swim all night, and he determined to stick to his plan. Then, he thought, when morning came he could hide among the rocks beside the river, and take to the water when darkness came again. "Did I really fool Cohonk?" he wondered. "The child was sure I was drowning—but was she? Or will she send someone to search for me, as soon as it is day?" He wished he knew the answer, but it was just as well that he did not.

Peter's head felt light. He became hot instead of cold, and he felt strange. "Must swim," he kept saying to himself, over and over. Sometimes he spoke aloud, but he did not realize it. Sometimes, he spoke in Indian. "Must swim. Must swim."

Peter did not know how feeble his strokes were becoming. Suddenly, he felt water close over his head. "I'm done for," he thought, as he struggled one last time. "I couldn't make shore now, if I tried." Then he saw a blurred something just ahead. He reached out, and his fingers clutched at sodden bark. He had

164

found a log, floating in the water. With a sigh, he put an arm around it, and rested his cheek on its rough surface. Now he could keep his head above water without swimming more than a very little. Peter felt a ray of hope once more.

Long before Peter found the floating log, the three pinnaces and the Dutch trading vessel had sailed safely down the Pequot River. Endicott was on his way toward Boston and had already begun to write his report on the expedition. He made himself out to be pretty much the hero. But he forgot to mention that he had left the Saybrook men in the lurch. (Lion Gardiner wrote about that many years later.) Endicott had forgotten all about the little boat which was carrying corn. That shallop was still in the Pequot River, and night had closed in upon it. No one cared, except the men in the shallop, and they knew their lives were in danger!

At first Thomas Hurlburt and his companions had followed the pinnaces as fast as they could row their boat. But the bigger ships sailed well. They were soon out of sight around a bend in the river, and the shallop could not catch up. The Indians, watching from behind trees along the shore, saw this, and they began to shoot at the Saybrook men. Hurlburt was all right; he wore a steel corselet over a tough leather coat, and a helmet, but Joseph Daniels, who was steering, had no armor. An arrow pierced his shoulder, and he let go the tiller. The boat swung about wildly in the current, and before William Chace, who sat nearest, could grab it, the boat rammed her nose tightly between two rocks on a small island. There it stuck fast. The savages gave a howl of glee, but one of them ventured into the open, and Hurlburt had the satisfaction of putting a ball through him. Fortunately the island was very small—just a few rocks jutting up from the bed of the channel. Had it been one of the large islands near the mouth of the river, where the Pequots had established a village, the case would have been hopeless. Hurlburt and his men realized that the accident was serious enough, as it was.

"Shove aside the corn in the bow, John, and see if she's stove in," directed Hurlburt.

Hawks obeyed. "No, sir," he reported.

"Good," Hurlburt exclaimed. "Then we have a chance. Take an oar, and see if you can shove us off. Ed, you watch the west bank, and if you see a Redskin, fire, but don't miss, my lad. We haven't all the ammunition in the world, you know. I'll take care of these beauties over on this side. Joseph, you're not killed. Stop groaning, and try to help us shove off, can't you?"

But shoving off was easier said than done. The men heaved, and swore. Finally Hurlburt handed his musket to Daniels, who was more scared than hurt, and had begun to recover his nerve. He then climbed out on one of the rocks. This lightened the shallop, and with a few mighty heaves, he and the others got her off. He clambered back with difficulty.

The delay was serious, however, for now, it was beginning to grow dark. "We must anchor in midstream," Hurlburt decided. "We can't risk getting stuck like that again. The woods are full of savages; we wouldn't have a dog's chance."

"Suppose they come out in canoes?" suggested Joseph Daniels, who was newly arrived in America, and very nervous.

"We'll keep a watch, of course," Hurlburt said. "There aren't many good canoes left on this river, don't forget. But we'll look sharp, and if you go to sleep young man, I'll scalp you, myself, without waiting for the savages to do it." He grinned as he spoke, and Daniels grinned back, for Hurlburt was a likeable fellow and a fine leader. They settled themselves for the night.

At last, the first gray streak of dawn appeared in the sky. Out on the river, away from the trees, there was already a good deal of light. It was not Hurlburt's turn to watch, but he felt his sleeve pulled, and awoke instantly. "What is it, Joe," he whispered. "See something?"

"I dunno," answered Daniels, his teeth chattering in the early morning cold. "Might be a beaver. Might be someone swimming." He pointed, and Hurlbut saw a dark head. As it drew near, he could tell it was indeed someone swimming, very feebly.

"Watch out," Hurlburt said. "Maybe it's a trick. It's dawn —favorite time for Indians to attack, I'm told." He thrust out an oar. "Ahoy there," he said. "Where going!"

Peter saw the oar as a sort of vague blur. Instinctively he reached out and clung to it. Faintly familiar words reached his ears, as though from a long distance. "Ahoy," he said. "What ship, sir?"

"Why, it's a boy," exclaimed Thomas Hurlburt. "Here, give us a hand, Joe. The child's done in. He's nearly drowned."

They managed to pull Peter into the boat, where he sank to the pile of cut corn, almost unconscious. "Is it a Pequot?" asked the other men, who had wakened.

"Dunno," said Hurlburt. "Looks like an Indian, but he talked English just now. Look at his back—all bruises. Whoever and whatever he is, he's not been treated so well."

"Must hide," murmured Peter. "Daylight—must hide."

"There you are—English!" exclaimed Joe Daniels. "We'll

"The child's done in—he's nearly drowned."

hide you, lad, don't fret," he said, kindly. "He's half out of his head," he told the others.

They made Peter as comfortable as they could in the bottom of the boat, partly covering him with bags of corn to please him, for he still insisted he must hide. "And we must be off," declared Thomas Hurlburt. "The boy is right—it's day. Up with the anchor. We can see the rocks all right, now. Let's get out of this river as fast as we can."

When, a few hours later, the Pequot trackers searched the river banks, they found no traces of the little slave. Some friends told them that a shallop with white men had passed, but there was no boy with them, they said. Only corn.

20: PEQUOTS ON THE WAR PATH

WILLIAM JOB rose early and strolled outside the Saybrook fort. He had persuaded Eliza Coles to give him some breakfast, but as usual, he felt he had not had enough to eat. "Why did I ever leave London to come to this God-forsaken spot," he thought. Then he looked at the little log fort he had built for Lieutenant Gardiner. There it stood, square and sturdy on the bluff. Job felt a surge of pride. " 'Tain't much, beside the Tower o' London," he thought, "but I'd like to see anyone build a better one with the material we had to hand." He crossed the open square to the stockade, and paused to thump the great logs, set deep in the ground. "Solid as a rock," he muttered. He spoke to the sentry, who let him out the gate. Far out upon the sound, he saw a tiny sail. "Our shallop's coming, as I live," he exclaimed.

The Dutch trading vessel had arrived the night before. When Hurlburt's men in the shallop failed to appear, everyone at the fort began to fear the worst. They were bitter against Endicott for breaking his word and taking no care of their men. The situation was all the harder to bear because there was nothing they could do about it.

Job glanced back at the fort. Should he go and tell the lieutenant the shallop was coming? No, he decided. "Maybe those bloody savages have murdered half our men. Better wait and see."

The rising tide brought the shallop into the Connecticut before very long. "Lend us a hand, Will," called Hurlburt, as he cast a rope on shore. "We've been chased by Indians all night."

He said this with his usual hearty grin. Poor William Job was afraid of Indians, though he tried to conceal it. His solemn face turned pale, and Hurlburt could not resist the opportunity to make sport of him. "Hurry," he cried. "The Indians are right on our heels."

The other men chuckled, but Job tied up the boat, and then reached for a bag of corn, as though there were not a moment to spare. Then he dropped the corn with a yell of fright. "Look," he gasped. "There's an Injun right there in your boat. Look out!" He pointed at the sleeping Peter, while everyone roared with laughter.

Peter awoke, and sat up. For a moment he could not remember where he was, or what had happened. Then he looked at the red sandy bluff, with the stockade at the top, and he recognized Saybrook. He did not stop to marvel at his good luck in finding himself in the very spot where he wished to go. He simply jumped out of the boat, and started up the path.

"Look out!" shouted William Job. "He's getting away. After him, boys!" In this imagined emergency, Job suddenly felt very brave. He himself sprinted after the fleeing Indian, with the idea of capturing him single-handed.

Job did not have to run very far. Peter was almost fainting from hunger, and only his determined spirit carried him forward. When he felt a hand on his shoulder, he turned. "Why, hello, Mr. Job," he said.

Poor William Job had never suffered such a shock in his life. His hostile Indian, whom he was pursuing with such bravery, had just turned around and called him by name! It was too much. He took out his handkerchief and mopped his brow. His jaws worked, but he could not speak.

Peter sat down on a rock for a moment. "It's funny," he said apologetically, "but my legs seem awfully wobbly. I've got to hurry, too. No time to lose."

Job looked at the boy again. Then something in the cocky little tilt of his head, some hint of fire still gleaming from Peter's dark eyes, made Job remember. "Why, it's that little limb of Satan, Peter Cutler," he cried. "What do you mean, dressing up like an Indian and scaring honest folk?" Then he looked more closely. "I declare, the lad's done in! Well, it beats the Dutch—but here we go." He raised Peter in his strong arms and carried him up the hill and into the kitchen.

"Some food, Eliza," he bellowed. "Look sharp, wench. Get porridge."

"Food, is it?" exclaimed Eliza Coles, turning away from the big fireplace. "You great hulking pig, I gave you your breakfast hours ago." Then she saw Peter, and gave a little scream. "Lord save us! An Indian!"

"Don't be ridiculous," said William Job, loftily. "Is your eyesight failing you, that you can't see who this is?"

Before Peter realized quite what was happening, he found himself seated at a great rough-hewn table. A wooden bowl of porridge was placed before him. "But I must see the lieutenant at once," he protested. "It's important, really it is. The Indians are coming. They're going to attack!"

To his amazement, William Job roared with laughter, and slapped his thigh. "That's good," he declared, "but don't try to catch me that way again. That's what Tom Hurlburt told me, down at the wharf. I was fooled once, but not any more. I know it's just a boy's foolishness, now."

At this point, Gardiner entered, followed by Thomas Hurlburt. "You've done a good job, Hurlburt," he was saying. "I want to congratulate you on getting your men out of a tight place. It's a fine load of corn, too, but what's all this about a sick Indian? Surely the Pequots didn't treat you so well that you wanted to adopt one and bring him home for us to feed?"

Hurlburt colored slightly. "It's—that is—well, we're not so sure that he is an Indian." Then he saw Peter. "There he is now, sir. Perhaps he can explain."

Peter managed to stand up, although he felt a sudden wave of dizziness. It was as well he could not see himself. He had lost his moccasins in the river, and he wore nothing but the breech skin that Cohonk had given him. His dark hair was long and tangled. His skin was as brown as an Indian's, but his ribs stuck out because he had been so poorly fed. This strange little scarecrow saluted, and said, "Peter Cutler, sir, at your service."

Suddenly, there was a rustle of skirts behind him, and a cry, half of joy, half of pity. To Peter's intense embarrassment, he found himself folded in a lady's arms, being kissed, bear's grease, dirt and all. He found himself looking into Mary Gar-

173

He raised Peter in his strong arms, and carried him up the

hill and into the kitchen.

diner's lovely face. He blushed, but he felt very happy.

They tried to make Peter eat a little before they would let him tell his story. But the good porridge seemed to stick in his throat. He took a sip or two of milk, the first he had tasted in many months. "Please let me talk," he said. "I'm so tired, I'm afraid I'll go to sleep."

"He's right," exclaimed Mistress Gardiner. "He needs sleep more than anything. He is so nearly starved that we must give him only a little food at first. Tell us your news, Peter. Then I will put you to bed."

Peter told all he knew of the Pequots' plan to attack Saybrook. He told of secret councils he had heard in the Indian town. But before he was half through, Lieutenant Gardiner jumped to his feet.

"Sergeant Willard," he cried, "have the drummer beat for assembly. Did two men go down to the garden?"

"Yes, sir."

"Well, send sentries to guard them. Sentries to look sharp for savages, understand?"

Lieutenant Gardiner came back to Peter. "How soon will the Pequots go on the war path?" he asked. "Will they wait to make a treaty with the Narragansetts?"

Peter shook his head. "No, sir. They feel sure the Narragansetts will burn Boston, if they set them the example by burning Saybrook Fort. They are so aroused over General Endicott's attack that the whole tribe must be on the war path by this time."

Lieutenant Gardiner began to pace the floor. Outside, on the parade ground, the men were mustering. There were pitifully few, even as Sassacus had told the Pequot warriors. "It is just as

176

I foresaw," said Gardiner, half to himself. "Endicott came here to this fort first, before he set out for the Pequot River. He was wind-bound here four days. Here he stayed, his men eating up our little store of food, while he told me how simple it would be to subdue the Pequots. 'You will only raise these wasps about our ears,' I told him. 'Then you will sail away to Boston, where you think you are so safe. And you will leave us to be roasted at the stake, or to starve.' "

Peter felt the room sway about him. He jerked his head up, knowing he had almost fallen asleep. "Come, Peter," said Mistress Gardiner. She took him by the hand, and led him to her own cabin, just north of the soldiers' quarters. She and Eliza Coles heated water over the fireplace, so that Peter could wash the dirt and bear's grease from his thin body. They cut his tangled hair. Then they gave him one of Lieutenant Gardiner's linen nightshirts, and put him into the big four-posted bed. All of this he realized only vaguely. His mind was full of confused pictures of recent happenings.

For a time, he slept. Then the brass cannon on the watch tower spoke, and Peter sat up. "The Pequots! I must tell Lieutenant."

Mistress Gardiner's soft voice calmed him, and he remembered. "They are attacking, Peter. But we are ready," she assured him. "Look, it is night. All the settlers have reached the fort in safety, thanks to you. The Pequots burned our cornfield, but we cut and carried away many bushels before they came— all thanks to you."

"I don't understand," said Peter. "How could all that happen by night-time?"

"Two days have gone, Peter. You dreamed. You talked.

177

Sometimes you imagined things, and I called our good Dr. Pell, because I was worried about you. Don't you remember? He came, and said you simply needed rest. Then another man came, someone who loves you very much. Do you remember, Peter?"

Peter shook his head. "I think I remember saying some silly things," he said, a little ashamed. "I thought I was a slave again."

Mistress Gardiner came over to the bed. She had a bowl of steaming broth in her hands. It smelled wonderfully good, and Peter drank it all. "Now rest again," she said. "You have done your part in saving Saybrook. Trust Lieutenant to do the rest."

Peter sank gratefully back among the pillows. He slept for a long time. When he awoke again, it was still dark, but through the oiled paper window by the bed, he saw a dull red glow. "Fire!" he cried, springing out of bed.

No one answered. Then he saw by the embers on the hearth that the cabin was empty. He pushed open the heavy oak door, and ran outside.

21: PETER CUTLER OF SAYBROOK

AS soon as Peter opened the cabin door, the smell of wood smoke came to him clearly from the north. He turned, and saw the palisade looming black against a dull red sky. Peter breathed a sigh of relief. At least, the fort was not on fire, as he had feared.

He started to cross the parade ground to mount the wall for a better view. Then he stopped in astonishment. The little square, which had been empty when he first reached the fort, was now crowded with people. He could see them dimly, crouched in silent groups around small camp fires. Piles of household goods lay about them. There were a few horses. There were hens and

179

chickens in improvised pens. Peter began to pick his way among them. Then he understood. These were the settlers, who had fled from their clearings. Because of Peter's warning, they had reached the refuge of the fort in time. He noticed that only women and children were there. The men must have been posted at the palisade.

Peter saw a torch burning beside a narrow flight of steps leading to the north watch tower. He promptly climbed the stairs, and found himself on a platform beside a small brass cannon. Men stood beside the cannon ready to fire, but no order came, because the enemy was too far away. A new blaze sprang up a trifle to the westward. "There goes my home," said one of the men, with a groan. "We had just finished it in time for cold weather."

From the watch tower, a narrow platform ran the length of the palisade walls, about six or seven feet from the top. This was to enable sentries to pass all around the fort. Loop-holes had been cut in the wall at intervals. These were guarded by men with muskets. A man approached, and Peter recognized the resolute bearing of Lieutenant Gardiner. "May I have a musket, sir," said Peter. "Where shall I stand guard?"

Lieutenant Gardiner turned, and peered into the darkness. The flickering torchlight from below picked out a scarecrow of a boy with a man's nightshirt trailing almost to his heels. "Why Peter Cutler, go back to bed," exclaimed the lieutenant.

"Yes, sir," said Peter.

Something in the boy's voice made Lieutenant Gardiner add hastily, "You've done your part, boy. Don't worry about the fort. I have plenty of men, now that the settlers are here to help me."

Peter turned obediently. He was bitterly disappointed. Once more, the man he had always wanted to serve had refused him. "I shall never be one of Gardiner's men," he thought, "no matter how hard I try to please him." He noticed for the first time the ridiculous way in which he was dressed, and his cheeks burned.

A voice spoke at the foot of the stairs by the watch tower. "Did someone say, 'Peter Cutler'?" The voice sounded half hopeful, half afraid. Peter ran down the steps. He saw a tall boy carrying a bag of powder. "Sam!" he cried. "Sam West!"

The next thing he knew, the boy had dropped the powder, and was pounding him on the back. "I thought the Pequots had got you, Peter," Sam cried. "I thought you were dead!"

Suddenly Peter began to laugh. "And when you saw me in this white thing, you thought I was a ghost, I'll wager!"

"I'd know that sudden laugh of his, anywhere," thought Sam. "It's my Peter all right." He said, "I came up the Pequot River to look for you, Peter. They wouldn't give you up. Then Red Fox found out for sure where you were, and we were going back again when the alarm came. Our family got to the fort just before the Pequots struck."

"Then you're all safe!" cried Peter joyfully. "And you never forgot me, Sam?"

"Oh I might have known you'd get away from the Pequots all by yourself, you old Wunx," Sam said.

"I'm afraid I wasn't as foxy as you think," said Peter, remembering the times he tried to escape, and failed. It did his heart good to hear the old nickname again. "How is Sally?" he asked eagerly.

"Where is that boy with the powder?" interrupted a stern

181

voice from the head of the stairs.

"Coming, sir," said Sam. "Sally's well. I'll tell her you're here," he called back to Peter, as he ran up the stairs. Then Peter remembered that he, too, was under orders—to go to bed!

The sun was just rising when Peter heard Eliza Coles stirring up the fire. "Here is something for you," she said. "A pretty little Miss with big gray eyes came by with this bundle. She says these are some of her brother's clothes for you to wear."

"That must have been Sally West," exclaimed Peter. He put on the suit of homespun. How glad he was to be dressed like an English boy again!

"Now lend me a hand with the trestles and the board," said Eliza. "The Mistress is out among the settlers. She is bringing friends of yours here, and she has ordered a fine breakfast. So set around the porridge bowls; there's a handy lad. Make a nice bow for the gentle folk, when they come in, the way you used to do in London. Or have you forgotten proper ways among those heathen savages?" Eliza added, her voice softening a little.

"Indeed, I have not forgotten," said Peter, making her a mockingly low bow as he spoke. "Why are you so anxious over my manners all of a sudden? Who is coming, anyway?"

"That I will not tell," Eliza answered.

Lieutenant Gardiner entered the cabin, followed by his wife. He sank into a chair with a sigh. "Well, my dear, nearly all the settlers have just sailed on the *Rebecca* for Boston," he said. "We have fewer mouths to feed, and I am thankful. But I wish more men had volunteered to stay and help defend the fort. Are you sure you should not sail back to Boston, when another barque comes?"

"Sam," he cried, "Sam West!"

"Indeed, I will not go," replied Mistress Gardiner with spirit. "I will stay with you. I will load muskets, and fire them, if need be."

Lieutenant Gardiner looked up, and noticed Peter for the first time. "You're looking as good as new, lad," he said. "We'll soon put some flesh on those bones, even if rations are short hereabouts."

Peter took firm hold of his courage. "This is the last time I'll try," he said to himself. "I hear you need recruits, sir," he said. "Now I can load a musket, and I would soon learn to shoot straight."

He saw a twinkle in Lieutenant Gardiner's frosty eyes. "Can you still polish boots and clean saddles?"

"Indeed I can, sir."

"Well, Peter, I am very happy to have you. You are nearly fourteen, I believe. That's young in years, but you have learned the soldier's first duty, as I saw last night. You can obey. The pay is poor and uncertain, Peter. The chances of seeing action are rather too good. However, if you wish, you may sign the articles of war. You may become a soldier, serving the Lords and Gentlemen."

Peter could hardly speak for joy. His dream had come true, at last. "Oh, thank you," he managed to say. "Would I really be one of your men?"

"Here's my hand on it!" replied the lieutenant. "Report to Sergeant Willard in an hour's time."

Lieutenant Gardiner turned to his wife. "I see you are expecting guests." They exchanged a glance, as though they shared some pleasant secret. "I must eat and go," he said. "Please make my excuses."

"I'm sorry," she replied. "I hoped you would see them together."

When the lieutenant had gone, Peter suddenly remembered something. "Mistress Gardiner," he said. "I have really come to Saybrook, as I promised you I would. May I have my mother's miniature? I think I can keep it safely, now."

To Peter's great surprise, Mistress Gardiner seemed distressed. "I haven't it, Peter," she exclaimed. "Yesterday, when you were so ill, I—I gave it to someone."

Peter could not understand. He wished he had not spoken. He was bitterly disappointed because the miniature was gone. "What a strange thing," he thought. "Why doesn't she explain!"

Just then there was a knock on the door. It was Sam, his sister, and a tall man with graying hair. Peter thanked the Wests for the suit of homespun he was wearing. "I thought I would need to make it smaller for you," said Sally. "But it fits well enough. You have grown tall since—since—" (She hated to mention Peter's captivity. It must be a nightmare to him, she thought.)

"Since we hid in Captain Gallop's haymow?" suggested Peter.

"Yes," laughed Sally. "I would like to see our old friend, Captain Gallop, to tell him you are safe and sound, Peter. He took it greatly to heart that you were captured while in his service. He and Captain Webber are partners now."

While Sally was speaking, Peter noticed that the tall man was standing by the fireplace, talking to Mistress Gardiner in low tones. Peter had the feeling that they were talking about him, and he turned his head to look. He saw the man's expression

185

change. All the sadness in his face was swept away in a sudden look of joy. Peter's heart warmed to the stranger. "I would like to know that man," he thought.

"Come, children," said Mistress Gardiner. "I know you have much to tell each other, but we must eat our breakfast and go about our work." They sat down at the table.

"What do you think?" Peter heard Mistress Gardiner say.

"There can be no doubt," the man replied. "He has his mother's eyes. He has a quick way of turning his head that I remember well. There's a lift to his chin that he had, even as a child."

"Peter," said Mistress Gardiner—and he had never heard her voice quite so gentle before—"Peter, this is your father. He has come searching for you—all the way to the New World."

Peter looked into the face of the strange man seated at the table. Their eyes met, and Peter's heart felt suddenly warm and happy. "How do you do, sir," he said faintly—because Eliza had told him to mind his manners. He was glad he was sitting on a sturdy oaken settle, because his knees felt suddenly weak.

Robert Cutler drew forth a worn silver frame from his inside pocket, and showed Peter his mother's miniature. "You are very like her," he said.

Then Peter understood what Mistress Gardiner had meant when she said that the miniature was gone. He gave her a grateful glance. "Mother always said you would come for me, sir," he managed to say. "So this is how it feels to find a father," he thought. "I supposed I would be gay. Instead, I feel solemn and like crying, like a silly girl."

Fortunately Eliza Coles had placed hot food in front of everyone. It soon had its effect. They all began to talk. "I was so afraid

186

I'd tell the secret," cried Sally, laughing.

"Did you know, all the time?" exclaimed Peter.

"Oh yes. Mr. Cutler plans to take some land right next to ours. We shall be planters under the charter of the Lords and Gentlemen, Peter—our family, and yours."

Peter felt a surge of pride. Already, Lieutenant Gardiner's prophecy was beginning to come true: Peter Cutler, Esquire would have a home in Saybrook.

Then a cloud fell on the little gathering. "I mean we used to have a home here," said Sally. "The Pequots burned it last night."

"But I am one of Lieutenant Gardiner's men, Sally," said Peter.

"And I, too," said Sam.

"I, also, have joined him," said Peter's father.

"So we will hold the fort, Sally," Peter concluded. "Sooner or later, those Pequots will be conquered. Then we will build our homes again in peace."

By the time the meal was over, Peter felt as though he had known his father always. Now they must soon report for guard duty, but they lingered for one more word together.

"I am a farmer, my son," said Mr. Cutler. "I would be happy to have you follow in my footsteps. But I have talked to Captain Webber. He speaks well of you, and he tells me that you wish to follow the sea. Is that right?"

"Yes, Father," said Peter. "I will help defend the fort until the danger is over. Then I would like to get a berth aboard a trading vessel—if I may, sir," he added, remembering that he was no longer his own master, as he had been for so long.

His father smiled as he realized this curious change for Peter.

"You have a small account with a Boston warehouse, Peter," he said. "Your trading venture had already turned out well before you were captured. If you wish, you can buy a part interest in some vessel as soon as this Indian warfare is over."

"Could I buy an interest in the *Bachelor,* and ship aboard her again?" cried Peter.

"Captain Webber has already told me he would take you and train you for mate as soon as you are old enough." Peter's father smiled, but Peter saw the worn look come into his face again. Mr. Cutler added, "Captain Webber did not believe you would ever be found—when he said that. But he will be glad to keep the promise. Would that please you?"

Peter laughed. "Why, I have a father now, and a home in the New World. I'd be happy if I were just cabin boy again."